G. MERIDIAN PARIS

# CONFESSIONS

*The Love Story You Want To Feel…*

Learning How to Love Yourself Even When in One-Sided Relationships

AuthorHouse™
1663 Liberty Drive
Bloomington, IN 47403
www.authorhouse.com
Phone: 1 (800) 839-8640

Published by AuthorHouse  10/15/2019

ISBN: 978-1-5462-7794-1 (sc)
ISBN: 978-1-7283-0248-5 (hc)
ISBN: 978-1-5462-7795-8 (e)

Library of Congress Control Number: 2019901058

Print information available on the last page.

authorHOUSE®

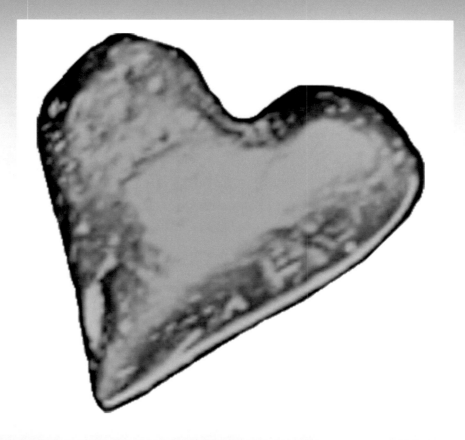

*To have an educated mind you must have an educated heart...*

G. Meridian Paris

# Contents

Sugar: Loosing The Addiction; Finding My Own Sweetness.....................................................1

WALKING ON GLASS ...........................................................................................3

Tolerance Dissipated, And Rediscovery.….........................................................5

The Band-Aid Effect ..........................................................................................7

Beginning to Love.… ..........................................................................................10

Ribbons, Laces, And Frills..................................................................................11

Roses, Tulips, And Calla Lilies...........................................................................12

Stunning Blue Irises...........................................................................................14

First Birthday; Again.….......................................................................................16

Alstroemeria & Rose ..........................................................................................18

Doves Of Love ...................................................................................................20

Harps And Orchids.............................................................................................24

Maple Leaves At The Foot Of The Bed .............................................................28

Swans Of Purity.................................................................................................30

The Shell: Protective Of Life, Love, And Self-Actualization........................................34

Lyrical Art, Oceans, Boat Rides, And Inspiration ....................................................39

The Elegant Purity Spoken And Creatively Unspoken From The Heart ..................42

Entangled Fingers Of Holding Hands: Of The Eternal Friendship
 and Eternal Love Of Prince Albert And Queen Victoria........................................45

THE ONE-SIDED RELATIONSHIP .........................................................................48

Constellation...........................................................................................................56

Art, Poetry, Gems, and Inspired Music...................................................................59

Claddagh-Synergy...................................................................................................67

Mesmerizing Gardens On A Plate And Healing Red Clay ......................................73

Productivity And No Holograms..............................................................................82

Cupid's Arrow Struck The Greek Apple...................................................................85

Lace Parasols And Intense Gourmet Chocolates................................................... 121

UNITED ENDEVOURES; ......................................................................................... 122

"Of course. And both very, very uncomfortable, but THE BEST PLACE IN THE, you know, HURRICANNE IS, like, IN THE MIDDLE OF IT." - Jay-Z

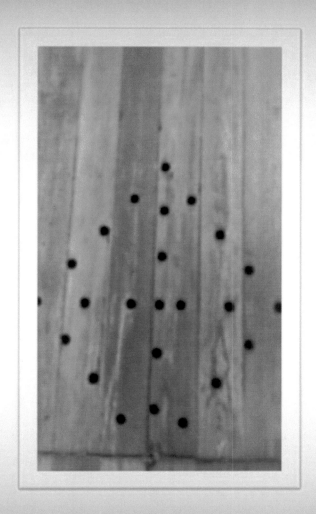

# Sugar: Loosing The Addiction; Finding My Own Sweetness

LOVE. What an interesting sentiment. It is an overwhelming elegant dance when you electrify this synergy with someone else.

Love is often associated with expectations and responsibilities that may or may not be accurate.

But can you love yourself tomorrow better than you love yourself today? Often, when we think of love we immediately think of another, the absence and expectations of the void that the another would fill, but not simply ourselves. If someone inquires, "do you love yourself" most immediately shrug an outburst of "of course I do". But, do you excite yourself because you woke up? Do you look forward to moments in the day that you will spend with yourself? This is beyond what you can do, to appreciate yourself is a level and this is a deeper level to that beginning. To care for yourself is a wonderful basic shallow end start. To take pride in what one can accomplish and push that to the most utmost limit is coming out of the shallow end.

So, Happy New Years! Happy Valentine's Day! Happy every day! Today is not just about how life incorporating you intertwined with the balance of others, today is also about you loving you!

# WALKING ON GLASS

When being determined that the house had to have every single item removed, either to donate, storage, or mostly to let go, some things broke. It was hard to watch that happen. Several times, I got glass in my feet, in my thigh once when I sat down, and so forth. It was not that we aimed for glass and it did not happen in every moment. It was that it was impossible to keep up with the fragments and to keep going on the pace that we were aiming for. It can be looked at as trying something new or an adventure for life's new page turner. The new chapter can be seen as a harmonic melodic concert. The beginning to the next ride of our lives. It may not be the only ride to take but at least preparing for the ride is the first step.

On one of the last days, I stepped onto glass. I did not fret at first, as it was not the first time and the mission was the focus. I was not able to get this piece of glass out and over time the glass in my heel made it hurt with every step. In the following days, others took the time to attempt to tweeze the glass from the swollen and sore location upon my heel. They could feel the knot but could not see the glass. Every touch streamed further pain through me. I withstood the added extreme shooting sharp pain in hope that each time would be the last and the glass would be removed. It was not only excruciating. Each time, they still did not remove the glass. I knew each step would hurt and could have quit. I could have quit and let go of the sweet dreams as the overwhelming situational blazes were breaking loose. I walked on this foot. I did not let it stop me. I checked it, I said occasional comments when it became almost unbearable. My tolerance was in determination. Some inquired if the forced situation of the circumstance made me clear out the amount that was cleared. No, it would have been easier to move it all into storage and not go through it. To not reveal to others how much had accumulated from fear

and time. Now, there is a tiny knot in the bottom of my foot. Some thought it would work its wa
out, but that theory only worked if I were not walking on it every day and in an enclosed shoe
And yes, often I began in shoes but due to cleaning, rain, lots of rain as winter was coming in
and other circumstances, often the shoes would come off. Once I even had on sock slipper
and the glass went through that. It was a magnetic hourglass. One of the children were boar
and kept trying to figure out how it worked. Of course, they broke it. They were sorry, and w
placed the two pieces onto the table to get it immediately out of their reach. The next perso
who came by in just moments knocked into it and the top part shattered across the floor. W
swept but could not find it all. Some shards were found when reaching for other items an
suddenly sharpness is felt in the side palm of the hand or such. That is not the piece that i
now wedged permanently into my foot behind scar tissue, for me to always have a reminde
but glass was everywhere and much of it just simply became destroyed in the process.

I knew from the glass around it that it was a thicker piece but not antique mirror or 1970
table glass thick. It does not pain me in each step but I yet to have to see the repercussions c
the glass remaining within my body. For now, it serves as a reminder. A reminder of how muc
has to be conquered, how painful it truly is, to reach the other side. Like a diet, yes, one ca
do fat freezing through lunch or other measures that may be necessary but unless they chang
a diet and begin to exercise at least somewhat to utilize the body, then the same behavior wi
render the same outcome. The same verdict may not be the goal if one is attempting to do fa
freezing or surgery. In my case, the pre-packing or getting rid of a few handful of things, an
a few trashcan loads, at a time. The first time I was aware of the problem, the first grocery tri
for two items ended up being an entire trunk for the place we stayed for a couple of weeks an
for the first temporary location. I had to remain tremendously aware after that not to transfe
one necessity area to another. I also reminded myself that no matter what pain emotionally
physically, or anything else that I was ever about to face, I was walking on glass, and then afte
all that it was worth reaching the next step. And as far as the glass, I touch the knot from tim
to time, but it does not shoot pain into me with every step anymore. I suspect this is what it i
like to reach each new phase of life. You must be willing to endure all that is dished, includin
walking on glass. It may hurt to make a change, but the effort is worth it. And improvement c
what we do know lets us begin to know what we do not know, what is next to reach for.

# *Tolerance Dissipated, And Rediscovery…*

Unlocking the power and knowing the existence of a problem, I came to realize are two separate things. To climb a mountain has to occur one step at a time. But the path may not be seen. I was stronger than I knew and had a voice that only others said was great. I did not know how to conquer and achieve what I believed was once and desired once again. How to feel the strength and being stronger than I even knew, where to begin? By being willing to take the step. By asking for help but putting more effort out than I even knew I could do. It was not just the physical, but also the mental levels. There are so many hours in a day. We reach for those things that are most important to us or is required for another goal, such as survival and prestige. I knew I did not want to turn back and some things, if I had taken longer to think about them, I would have held onto them longer. To self-maintain, to force a better step of oneself despite the obvious barriers and others doubts and believe me even in this situation there were doubters, is always worth the modification to what is important on a daily basis.

There is so much information online on every single subject or topic. Friends and family have opinions. One has to know the combination of measures that one desires to implement, stick to it, and utilize to make a difference. Also, at what pace does one accomplish the clear journey and path to be taken?

I recall a supporter becoming angry with me and providing an analogy. They told me of bein
a boxer in a boxing ring and that you have to be at that level to even compete with them in th
ring. I cried. My soul just withered, and I felt dismay. I felt as if I had to bring who I was u
that was true. I had done much to make that begin but had a long way to go. I felt that truly w
were walking on the same trail path. We were looking at the same changing season leaves, th
same frost on a pond, twirling in my own dance next to them and feeling the synergy throug
our climb. I also realized that one slows down to try to step into someone else's footstep
I never saw us as the same footsteps. Yet, supportive and moving with the same convictio
and on the same path in the same direction, yes. I cried that night. I lifted my head with a ne
light and his words and his beliefs that he always said regarding me as if they were bird sun
melodies in my heart. I had heard him often. I have not been able to listen. I was now able t
begin to shine my brightest light, but lights come in all settings, and I was New Year's excite
to find mine. I was lucky to have someone who desired to suggest to me instead of negativit
or pushing, until I actually could feel the meaning behind the words they were saying. It hu
more to hear them when they were occasionally negative versus anyone else because the
said something that many did not, and I did not know how to feel in order to believe, "Yo
are stronger than you know; I believe in you". It was the perfect personal gift. Sure, a flora i
gorgeous. It was a continuous gift from the heart. And they backed their words with action
The feelings behind it. The thoughts that went into it. The positivity of even the one commen
People say to surround yourself with positiveness. Sometimes, that is not an option. Sometime
situations are so overwhelming, just knowing what to admit without complaining can be hard t
find within ourselves. Sometimes, people know the problem, but they provide meaningless c
empty gestures because they do not know what else to do, negativity may be more partial t
their nature, or they are overwhelmed by the matter and cannot bond with it. If the environmer
is toxic, reach online for uplifting, reach within oneself despite any environment and then decid
what you desire for tomorrow. How can that be reached? Seeing tomorrow is taking today t
reach that visual. Then, what is the first step to take? Even if that step takes a year, stay focuse
the first step is the hardest.

# The Band-Aid Effect

Doing it all at once can be fine and good but it does not resolve most internal issues. Just with any wound, it needs time and reevaluation. With any band-aid, quick removal of anything stings. As with anything underneath that band-aid, the purpose would have been to cover, protect, provide time, or a barrier directly to the wound that needs healing. If removed all at once and not during or after the beginning of healing, it may be more harmful than helpful. Some mention in pride of going cold turkey. Yet others mention doing a New Year's resolution that only made them worse in a couple of months. There must be a balance.

So, once when one child was young, their forward-thinking parents decided not to whip them. The parents decided that they would wrap empty boxes at Christmas and when the child acted up, they took one and threw it into the fireplace fire. Tears flowed, and more than the message would be received. When it was summer, the parents would take a select one of the child's birthday gifts, fuss and storm, then toss it into the lake behind the house. It was not for years until the child discovered what the truth was. It created serious baggage. It was not until the child was much older into adulthood that they met a counselor that helped them gently unpack that baggage. It was because the now adult (the child) went shop crazy for things that they did not utilize during the year while having a seeded hatred for the two significant times of the year. Their significant other thought that they would create a surprise since they were about to move in together. The significant other hired someone to move all the things that were not in use out and thoroughly clean the place. It was in positive thought and they knew that the insurmountable amount of things would not be conducive to a positive atmosphere. The significant other proudly then had movers help move in the things that mattered for them. Everything had a place and the significant other could breathe and thought they had done a grand thing. The person that mattered to them would not have to lift a finger and, two birds with one stone, the two of them could look at the future from the newly condensed, purged and merged location.

Unfortunately, it only ripped the band-aid from the underlying causation of the problem. It was not until he worked with a specializing counselor and that counselor provided him with perspective, self-acknowledgement, uplifting replacements for internal blockers and some steps to take that he agreed would work for him. Then the true healing and deep internal breathing beyond the immediate truly began. The significant other went livid when they saw that their love had gone binge shopping in emotionally responding to noticing that most of the things were gone. The component that boiled over within them self was that he had not had the option to go through his own things. Then, he reflected and calmly realized for the first time how this would impact his significant other. Although he defended it, he was more aware of what he had done and supported the one that he loved. He and his significant other together learned what the true triggers, limitations, and deep seeded reasons for the occurrences were. He discovered so much about himself when he allowed himself to learn and desired an outpouring instead of a syrup drizzle from the outside on top. He discovered what other areas of life he desired to enhance to support his overall well-being. Then, he pointed out that to tame the wild strand, to heal with self-trust, he had to lay his past and fears down. Truly addressing his insecurities through a spiritual path bound by intellect that is constantly renewed hence reducing inhibitors, secure enough to let go, and happy in each step of progression. In order to reach for the sky, one's hands, have to be empty. And to let go, one has to understand that to survive is a form of conquering. No one can replace the past but making it a testimony is a new wave of life by itself. Others may fill the holes with alcohol, eating, and innumerable other quick sand life functioning not feeling that hole type items. Replacing survival of the initial wound does not reveal more of life. It also impacts other parts of life. Although support is great, others cannot heal the wounds for another. They can share in the promise and the vision and walk the path hand in hand for as long or as short as it takes. The individual will know what coordination will begin to work for them this time that may or may not have worked the last time.

As these two discovered, the beginning 'walker' steps is not an easy step. It is painful and may take some work to learn to re-walk. One may never walk the same as glory day this or expectation of another. That is not the point. Even if they knew of someone or if they knew this individual when, they are really saying that they just want this individual functional and they do not know how to see them functionally acceptable. Even though it may work for some, most cannot be on the 'walker' one day feeling an airy numbness to being able to walk or run, finding and bridling the internal joy while accepting oneself. To accept oneself also means that one constantly reevaluates, is aware, and expands for positivity with improvement.

# Beginning to Love...

There's a flood of information available. For many areas of life, this can be tedious and discouraging. It is what is the beginning step to relighting one's own starlight and no longer thinking the darkness that surrounds us should impact that bright inner light. The sweetest smiles are the ones from the inside out. Those passions are genuine, and they are not contingent on what has occurred in life. Those are in the moment and depending upon how many moments are strung together. It is intense stretched without cruel pain and breathe memories or life in between. Smiles can occur in all places and at all times. They are not contingent upon finances or class bearings. It is a piece of bright light from the soul. The combination of what works is just like a smile. It just will. If rollerblading through the park is it, then strap up and go! If finding a new childhood because the one already lived was not worth mentioning, then circus, fairs, fishing, or opera for the weekend it shall be. Perhaps just helping with a foster home, boys and girls club, or big brother and sister program will be a much better manner of giving back and healing a time that cannot be repeated but survived regardless.

There were things recommended to me. There were things that I found to begin my steps.

# Ribbons, Laces, And Frills

First, there were flashbacks to things that I used to do and some that I never did. There were books of wonderful motivation. Then, there were very inspiring YouTube videos. Some were very intensive and motivational. Most were for reaching the goals that I desired. Some connected, some were exhaustive. The hardest step has been not to see myself through other's hypercritical comments. The negativity would come from so many different close sources that when I regurgitated what was said to me in repetition, it was thought that I held negative beliefs about myself. In reflection, when all was at a certain pace, and confidence was high, I still allowed those conversations. They just took very little time and did not consume in their impact.

With that same reflection, I realized, if someone was at Disney World and one cart was closed when someone desired a certain sparkly item, they would be disgruntled and perhaps comment. It would not matter that thy were in a unique attraction and each park is elegantly themed and designed with the utmost care. The same is seen when sitting at a grand wedding. Each detail was frighteningly critiqued instead of noticing the difference but enjoying the ride of the moment, respecting the wonderment of witnessing such an event, since one has chosen to be there regardless. If this is the typical case, then even the closest person may say the negative and not reinforce the positive that is already present.

# Roses, Tulips, And Calla Lilies

Yes, that negative may need to be corrected. I had to remember the positive that is not always spoken. Some of it is engrained since it was placed there from the beginning but just as taste buds, eyesight, body shape, and hearing can change, so does this. And who cares if the final outcome is perfect beyond someone else's measure. To allow someone to push beyond pushing sometimes can be a driver but I had to ensure that the undercarriage, the expectations, the focus, and the balance of positivity and negativity were of reaching the same goals for whatever the purpose. In the balance, I could not remove the adventure, the individual, and only focuses the goal. Yet betterment with nobility along the way is a goal that I will always strive for. I could not see drowning in only daily responsibilities. I came the conclusion that balance, focus, self-review, optimism, but most of all when a heart is broken or a situation, to not fear it healing differently then before. Not to dread the scar that will develop. Not to numb the pain or fill the hole before the scar with numbed grief or anxiety with any replacements. What happened to smell the roses along the way? What happened to loving the journey? It was not to say that I did not jot down goals, make steps to those goals, write in those steps other things that applied according to taking the measure. I took steps that pushed myself beyond where I was standing the day or the week before. That always reached for the light, even if the shadows blocked where that might be for this day. Supporting someone else helps their growth and blossoming, empowering. Yet somehow their smiles and light that escapes from underneath their darkness allows me to know that the little that I can do when I reach out, in truth, also reflects encouragement for their strength and light are strong in survival on their paths. But, to utilize my gifts for supporting and positivity. I know how it feels to be disheartened instead of encouraged and enlightened. It is exhilarating to help back and ironically healing.

If I became frustrated, I would copy a positive focused phrase in order to remind myself that I cannot take the same survival steps and expect a different result. I had to stay focused and keep myself paced in the positive direction no matter how hard. If I can only stretch at this part, I might be able to run a race, but a marathon is someone else's push. That is all that I had to realize. I still needed to thrust forward and with awareness; fearful of ever stagnant again.

Within this analogy, perhaps learn how to run that marathon but preparing for a race. The marathon runners might think that was weak or a waste but if I began off of a basic stretch, then conquering a race would be a major step. I desire a continuous race, not a short spurt. It should not be the only step that I ever take, or a satisfaction once complete, but I will not bash my soul in because I did not complete a measure according to someone else's plan or methods. Each determined single step in the right direction should make a difference and eventually change the course that was once set. Only positive attempts with positive goals! It is not a my way or the highway thing. It is accepting that it is okay not to measure up to someone else's plan and be a great me at the same time. That is still another way of not settling but seeing the positive and definitely beginning to feel the free of feeling the positive. It is refusing to sit back down onto the couch just because the first attempt may not have reached the final goals or feels so exhaustive as one is waking up from the numbness. It is like smelling the seawater or the flora for the very first time. It is doing whatever it takes to be sure you are okay and then the others that you love and care for. For single parents and others, often, it is sacrifice the majority of yourself first and hide or bury the pain and function first. Then, take care of what is left over. This is not opposite of that, just an even balance.

# Stunning Blue Irises

Then, I reflected upon something I would tell the children. I would tell them to love others for who they are, not for who they need or expect them to be. I would share for close family members or for even friends that would do or say things that they had to rise above and to stay emotionally above instead of absorbing. There will always be someone that we cross or interact with. Instead of them being the drill; we are a driving force, a positive, an uplift with hope and the capacity to change. As my youngest said, for a well-rounded person to respond in such measures or manners what truly is wrong with them, not me.

I considered consequences to any actions. If I did certain (above board) positions, it would impact my children. Children are not junior adults although some have responsibilities as such. Would the benefits justify the consequences? This always made a difference in steps made. As an adult, we can choose to leave most other adult scenarios and relationships. Some are more vivid than others. Some we cannot leave without duress in some form or fashion. For minors, they do not get the choice to have an active voice, yet they must learn to develop their voice and have love within themselves which is absolutely free. Just credit hours of life. I stand on the negative with positive. I stand on the awful or mistakes with everything that I have in me that is strong, good, and bright to take not just the first step but also the second. I will make consistent steps as not to sit on the sidelines of life, even if my pace or efforts are not the same to be measured up by any negative barrier. I ask them to reflect upon their decisions in moving forward as if they were at the three-quarter mark in life and looking back into the reflection of

your life. Did you love others? Did you make a difference beyond making a necessary hour's exchange of life for funding? Did you connect to the natural environment around you? Did you care for yourself in the best possible way? Did you depart from anyone if your paths were unhealthy or toxic but in a healthy way where both of your paths have a chance? And, a big one, did you love and appreciate yourself or numbingly give up on yourself as many highly functioning individuals can?

# First Birthday; Again...

There will be setbacks. So, every morning instead of jumping into the grind, I relearned how to meditate and how to spiritually prepare my way. Parents sacrifice themselves every day for their children. For their character, integrity and well-being. A few moments to make myself better makes that better. I then reflect upon the responsibilities and plan of each day. There were days that I had pains that would deter any attempt at the day that life had to offer. It was determination and motivation that ensured that day even occurred and that any part of it looked successful if achieved. Not every day is the same, therefore not every day has to mirror each other. As long as the attempt is not the last chapter in repeat.

If every year has a birthday, then what was achieved during that year? If every day is a new chance, what day is chosen to be the first step? And then the second? When I was younger I would write or type out situations to just clear them off my plate and be able to not hold them in congestion that I saw would occur to my associates through their waves of unforeseen circumstances. Now, the limited time in each day and other measures just seems to preclude this daily habit. I have seen others diary their best thought in the day as to not hold onto the bad, or to voice record every stage of a situation until it is complete and revisit some time later when the emotions are not drug into the thought process of it.

For me, on the first birthday after the release of items I desired to release and of some items I did not, those closest to me thought that a relaxing evening was intimate, personal, and what I should have as a gift since I just released lots of things. In thinking about it, considering the extreme stress and unusual timing of the birthday, I understood the gift. When I was fifteen

years younger, it was a time that taking baths by candlelight fit into the expected schedule. After each week of work at that time. This was the first time it was relaxing. A forgotten practice. I then found my rhythm of stretching and adding basic stretching or working out into my routine. With the encouragement of those closest to me, we may just take a walk, or go for a short hike. At one point in my life there were other activities that I used to do. I now faced whether I could still do them. It is that I am getting up for the starting line and knew that in trying for myself, I am trying for them.

One of my daughters cannot stand the thought of a bath so I got her a set of massage oils and an electronic neck massager. From now on it will be what they will do that will help them feel as nice as they desire me to feel in order to face the day. It does not take much. Just a transition. Music that would not normally be listened to for an active day.

In the simple steps, a bath, a warm up exercise, a meditative moment, I am rediscovering how I feel. I have to know how I feel in order to know what is next. Following other's judgements will not fulfill this rocky harsh climb. Supportive or just negatively commentate, I have to decipher beyond the silent numb that many have to some degree, including myself. It is feeling the inside of the wounds that the moment that they happened did not allow, as often it does not. Then other influencers will unintentionally either help along or distort the path. Someone with the right message at the right time could be all the encouragement that is needed to decide what step is the best step to take or to head towards. It is just that moment to think and to feel, feel what was already deep inside and needed to be acknowledged in order to continue to breathe appropriately. Encouragement comes from a vulnerable and belief location of others into yourself that can be very uplifting when positively received and then heard beyond listening. It is also to open the natural lock that we place on pain or wounds that develop into scars. Avoiding or numbing the pain is natural. Some people are talented enough to lock it away for years without immediate reaction, but it does not heal the matter and can manifest in other ways. It is how someone with an ulcer is amazed that they have one, but they work in high stress daily without a time to "smell the roses", decompress, more than a random alternate less stressful situation such as a once a year vacation.

# Alstroemeria & Rose

I had to accept that whatever was decided for the past has been decided and that is just learning not shame. It is awareness, not something else to hang my future head upon. I had to truly come to a point in the private swim or private walk with breathing and meditating to where it was released and not to be a source in conversation or action in the future. Not to say the events are erased. But who lives a perfect life? It is, "did I do the best I knew for the time"? "Can I fix from the point I am at in the future?" The past occurred. I can float on or that can be a stepping block to all possibilities for the future. Yes, the climb may be hard and treacherous. But, do I really desire to let that be my defeat, my merry go round until the end? How do I begin? Would I begin to decipher or journal all thoughts to include dreams, if not just to acknowledge them since that is also an essence of my raw truth and thoughts? Even if I cannot answer everything, it was discovering what to inquire of myself and being willing to rebound, recoil, and strengthen myself from the inside out. I recognized that when I did pick up the pace and was willing to take this to another step and another that it only will spill over in joy onto those around me.

I decided upon this road to self-improvement hand in hand with self-love for the benefit to those that are in my tiniest inner circle, mostly the short time, comparatively, that I have with my precious children.

Self-improvement and is a much longer road than just caring and open up within for self-love. As with knowing that putting certain foods and chemicals into the body will render an external

outcome, the same thing with how we nurture ourselves. And then hopefully hold compassion and nurturing for those around you. Only, when you are in survival mode, none of that matters. It is what is of gratitude in order to survive for the better good. It is what the moment renders.

I did not suddenly win the lottery. Life actually handed me worse first. I heard what others saw and the potential to light at the end of the tunnel that I was afraid to know was even there. To see my next step plan to just fully go away, and now have to develop a healthier one, one that allows the children to feel differently about themselves as so they hold their heads up as young adults leading .into adulthood. This is not over a few months. This was over a few years. They would have entered fully into adulthood if the pattern persisted with these circumstances. This was not neglecting them in any manner nor loving them any less. I ensured all that I knew to be best. It was that there was one element that impacted them and too much of anything, or too little of necessities, has always been said to be not a positive position to be in. self-love is not neglecting them. It is actually appreciating my strengths and abilities within a manner that I can address things on a stronger level and therefore become a daily more outpouring and uplifting person for them as well.

# Doves Of Love

In self-improvement, I had to acknowledge any possible toxic people that are around the family and how close to the family that they are. They are not dangerous, just toxic. Usually, these people are of the most sensitive or complicated measures. I do not know many but then again, I do not have a large circle. Most of the people that are in my circle are people of balance. People beyond balance, with wisdom and of genuine heart are unique and wonderful. But their path is theirs and knowing my self-improvement in order to continue to contribute in a stronger and better manner is only through the strength of my steps even if on the same path. As a family, we deciphered why the people may be toxic in this point in life, if we can help them, if it is possible to remove them or distance them from our life. It is not easy to change what others are used to from a relationship or situation. Yet, if it is not harmful and it is best, change can be necessary and good. Farmers do not typically grow the same exact crop season after season. They will rotate, rest the ground, or even burn the ground. It is not to say that that individual must change. There are so many options. How they are addressed, the kind of words spoken or how the interactions are thought of. So much can cause the "bright crop" that needs still to be tended to. If need be, no interaction, 'no crop' at all, might be called for in a healthier environmental approach. I must reflect and address if anyone ever felt this way towards myself at any point along the way and why as so I may be aware in strongly approaching a brighter and stronger tomorrow.

To notice other behaviors that came as a result, this was a time that I knew I must acknowledge the maple leaf of healing, feel the rose petal and tulip milky salt bath, and be healing in the truth of the origination, desire to be aware, with determination to change. I still appreciate to discuss and know the views that surround me from those on my same path. I heard so much negativity when I went from comfortable, not grand but comfortable, to meager. I appreciated the approval and acknowledgement. I went from confidence with subtle undertones to humbled and unworthy to overcompensating tomorrow every moment today. Since the children's survival depended upon me, everything felt like the storm had hit and I was preparing for the second half of it.

However, I do recall, one woman stated to me that she was a tracker. She was so insecure in her relationship that she was clingy with everyone. She was clingy with her boyfriend because she never had her father figure. She was clingy with his mother because she always interjected an obviously important opinion that surmounted her relationship and led the private conversations into arguments. She started seeing herself as her 'mother in law's' openly stated views of her that were more in fears than reality. She became clingy to even her co-worker and friend at work from desperate appreciation of approval. Lines were blurred from work dinners to desiring to have a friend to shop with or celebrate personal accomplishments. She knew she had gone overboard and was too clingy on everyone when her boyfriend got a job transfer and her company would allow her to telework for a move, but she literally began going into hyperventilation spells. It was no longer dominating decisions from the senior figure; her boyfriend would be off at work with her responsible at home. Her dynamics had changed. She realized then the unhealthy nature of the relationships she secured in her life and how she related to them. She did not end the relationships. She did not have the same underlying problems as I or the next person that heard her shout to glory. She decided to "grow up", as it is said. She changed what she saw to be unhealthy and acknowledge to the one that had to change it, herself. She began to lift her head and love all the bumps and curves, all the quirks and smarts, of the person that was looking back at her in the mirror; herself. To truly love oneself is to acknowledge oneself but to know that imperfection can be beautiful also accepting change is not admitting defeat. She repeated her desired outcome, she behaved and responded in ways that reached for her desired goals, until it was a part of her very muscle memory. She continued to review her goal setting through steps in the process. Another step? As determined as re-learning what to do after a horrifying first breakup, she discovered that navigating to avoid is not the same thing as taking it head on. Since she was continuously with the same people, and reestablishing the dynamics of their relationships, she also realized that it was like the recently quitting smoker at the mall entrances. For the enclosed malls, there still remained containers for the cigarettes to be put out before entering the mall or to dispose of trash in the receptacle. Time and time again, a smoker that is not currently smoking will slow down, pause, breathe deeply, and linger almost reminiscently in the unfortunate lingers that are at the main entrances and exits of the enclosed malls. Since her relationships were built in obedience and approval it was not easy for the transition firm enough that others as well respected this transition. It was easier for both sides to the equation to linger in the behavior, in reminisce, in the familiarity of the unhealthy behavior rather than just walking on in firmly past what used to be. Even more so, when she did this, when she was lingering negatively, she caught herself. She acknowledged her mistakes of the day or of the week. She listed everything that occurred, not just limited to her goals. She lifted her head up, acknowledged that she was human and figured out the steps that she honestly can take in those situations in the future. Then she outlined how she was going to keep things on track such as if she needed to state things to anyone or specify anything. Although she realized that this might have come across just as empty as a young child going up to another child stating that they were going to fight them while not doing anything beyond all of the words spoken. They were not on the path to be a 'Guido' when they grew up. She knew she had to do more than speak words. To step in her path and just inform those who may be caught off guard by the transition and that it really has no offense intended toward anyone else. Just a modification of growth and positive change. In acknowledging her position and thought process during the time, the body was functioning, but her pursuit was for other happiness first and no self-elevation less knowing any desire to discover oneself and love what she found. She discovered that she could forgive others as she acknowledged herself in the scope of the matters. Some had crossed some very abrasive lines in her life. She figured she would not hold it as a focus even if she was not ready to fully be in an honest forgiveness state of all matters. She would not live in it, cry in it, or provide time to whatever may have brought her to this state. She survived that. As for the rest. In acknowledging her role, who she was and may not be any longer, it helped her to release so much and truly and purely forgive from a broader and more thoughtful balanced point of view. She began to heal, learn, and then love the version of her that was stepping into the presence and then future with her.

# Harps And Orchids

This may seem like a broken record, but there are certain foods, certain chemicals, and certain situations in your life that can create an overflow of negative feelings within oneself. Some of those feelings may be tied to the medications that one is on, or it may just be perspective. There may be negativity in the situation. A dangerous place to live, being passed over, yet, it is a place to live and focusing upon a plan to reaching the safer place to live while also taking steps to make that place a safer place to stay, and at least still having a job while deciding on staying or applying elsewhere. Everyone can be broken. But how many can heal and know strength despite the worst, building upon the frazzled, truly knowing the wonderment within themselves, taking what little possibility of today and spinning it into the warmth and clothing tomorrow with all possibilities from the small strands of today? Many hear the words, feel the derogatory of circumstances, and dive into the pool drinking from it. Since drinking from it is not drowning, now is time to shed and strengthen.

Once, a child looked into a brush and said "Oh no! My hair!" I smiled and looked into their gentle eyes and said, "we all shed some hair. You are perfectly perfect, this is not anything atrocious to worry about. We have options to regrow that hair how we take care of the hair that is there. If it does not grow back, that was what was meant to be. But, for your sweet head, sometimes a little tingle or pain when we comb is only giving exercise to the roots for more hair to come in. Rub your fingers around, see, it is just a little bit from here and there where it needed to come from. You tiny one will grow the hair back in where it needs to be when it is time for it to be. It will cycle as such unless your body needs that strength elsewhere" The thought, analogy, crossed my heart. Just as the beauty in a sunshine ray or a windchime, as we tend to a garden we also tend to our hair. Now, there can be heredity or health to counter this claim. But generally, we tend to our hair. There are small parts that must come out. The hair will shed, knots be removed, dead ends in general, and so forth. It creates a healthier head. The same goes for placing generic perspectives upon the experiences and stumbling blocks that keep us from moving forward. In letting go, in accepting the scars developed into a new beauty, a new form of whom one is instead of seeing it as damage or destruction of whom one used to be, then it increases the strength and opens the heart to allow the new growth, the new abilities to areas of life or a vivid focus that probably was not the prior in-depth prior view; such as VHS to DVD to 3-D. There is no room for vividness if the pain of the scars or the living because of the scars instead of knowing that there is a strength in surviving and growth in order to have those life's scars.

You may already know what makes your DNA mix up to this point. But those people, as proud of you or unknowledgeable as they may be, had to live their own lives for their time and day. You get to decide what fascinating future lies from the fact that your DNA chain flows through you. Want your message to be different than where you are now? Can you find any positive about where you are? And now, build out from that your plan A, B, C, and D to get to the next step. Why so many? Because often when plan A fails, the entire plan fails.

Ask yourself questions of where are you desiring to be in five years, and if it is at the end of your life, and you are reflecting back, do you love the person that you see and does that depend upon someone else? You can love deeply and truly all of those that life directs into your hearts path. However, it does not deem that your love of self is dependent and not separate from love shared with others, even if others are a part of yourself.

A question that I inquire is, "if we picture our lives as a spreadsheet, the average life is 71 years. Break that down. That is 621960 hours. Now, if you were out of hours, reflecting back, did you accomplish anything that you desired to accomplish, and how many of those hours did you honestly, truly, and purely love, within the only chance that you are given; yourself?

Traditionally we are taught, from permission from parents, approval of friends and associate cohesiveness as a co-worker, requirements as a spouse, being a parent, and interactions wi offspring, that love is a reflection of gratitude or approval through someone else's eyes. This only one fragment of the complete gem that you are. This is also why it is so damaging whe one has experienced that portion of life and it changes or permanently alters. Not the on "why", but a portion of "why".

There are also expectations in every layer of the gobstopper of life. Expectations to eve level of education. Expectations to wherever one may live. Expectations from each interactiv relationship. Expectations from work or careers whether self-institutionalized or established b another entity that one strives to continue to excerpt. Expectations of society. Expectations fro groups such as friends, associations, religious affiliations, family traditions, and so forth. Th list could continue on. It is when life does not meet the current expectations or understandin of fitting oneself into those expectations that actually feels like a failure. We have so mar examples of single shining lights being the brightest. Of lives being touched by those wh knew their difference was a significance not the burden that others would have one believ This can come in all shapes and sizes to match what makes the difference. Like a lava lam the puzzle that needs pieces to fit, keeps on changing. However, ironically, it is not until the is a majority of those pieces that society desires to even recognize that the pieces need place to fit. Accepting a change in an expectation that one has strived for, will leave a scar. Ye being frozen and stating that things would have been, could have been, should have been, not accurate either. The rest of the parts to an individual and those that surround them kee developing. It is believing that what you invested your time and energy into would have bee better if. It was probably worth going down the path that you did for the time that you did. Wort it to the others on that path. Worth it to you. Is it worth it now to stay frozen for a path that do not currently exist? There can be one tree with many branches, so nothing is to say that th desired outcome is not also waiting on another branch, but you must keep going forward know. Fruit is very wonderful in its prime. No matter how long you try and hold onto the fru it will begin to decompose in its own time. If you plant the seed from that fruit and tend to invest time and energy into that fruit, then there is a possibility that you might possibly render more fruit in great time. It is accepting the change of the expectation and believing in yourself that there is more than the expectations that you once had. It is knowing that the purest cannot be replaced nor expected to. To move onto another expectation is only planting a seed, and although never the same, once weeded, watered, tended to, might render an outburst of return upon you. To continue to know that loving oneself and appreciating where one's life has been with a true focus of where one is going is worth the best attempt possible. All of who is a part of that journey will appreciate that of you and themselves.

# Maple Leaves At The Foot Of The Bed

To love yourself beyond just acknowledging your accomplishments or appreciating yourself, you must get lost in your maze. You have to find the middle, your heart, and then find your way out again. It's very easy to get lost in your maze. Most will spend more time with what they do, what skill set they utilize on a daily basis that they receive funding for, and dislike solitude for self-love, who they themselves are or desire to be, and happy discoveries that can reoccur at any age. It is a natural suppression of desire to have a partner or another's approval of whom one might be in life at this point. This is not to discount that. This is to state that often, that is the only love seen. Not the purest love, the love of self. To slow down, feel or learn internally, occasionally one will frustratingly see the convex and concave carnival mirrored view and run to the external comfort zone. There is so much to love in there even if it must be from a different pace from whatever known pace in the past. Realize that the future, the painting, bursts with many beautiful sources to its colors. It explodes with many different excitements of all levels and all paces. All of those colors have roots into the past but are never the same as the past. The future holds all that one is willing to give it. Only, how much of it is just baggage from yesterday that just needs weeding or brushing? This change can occur from innumerable sources.

Self-love is not egotism. This is not the wholesome knowledge of everything and belief that one and one's capabilities is always and already better than anyone else's along with even having to interact with others. Self-love is a balance and so much more. Too much or sprinkles of too little of anything is out of balance. The same would render of how one sees and loves themselves. If one walked around criticizing themselves and believing that they cannot do something because it takes a little more than they are used to, then that is an overdose of negativity and leads to impossibility. The one-sided relationship begins within. Then another outside of us can only receive in connection what is offered from within. It is not just remembering who you are or have been. It is using the skills and passions of who you are, scars and all, and reaching the best selves. Then, if desired, sharing that best self.

In celebration of who you are now, and the harmonic song of whom you are determined to be! Light your own internal flame and shoot that arrow towards the stars like fireworks!

A celebration of the legend that you will be and the whole person that you are including the scars. Scars are parts of you that must be connected to heal the damage that made a hole in the first place. Never to be the same, not to be accepted as always worse, just a different and sometimes harder path with a happier awareness because of the ability of survival. Only a baby can possibly be born in perfection and sometimes not even then. Often, we feel the loss, we move on but can only see what greets the world instead of the strength and power of what made us move on even if still not yet to overcome.

Love, one of the strongest, purest, silk wrapping emotions, can also flow from the inside out for ourselves along with anyone else or no one else. Celebrate what the future will be even if there is a darkness over each single step. If the end goal is seen, and the steps are known to exist, it is just taking each step one at a time, even if in total darkness and some disbelief.

You yourself can be the light that gleams that path even if it is shallow and twining up life's mountain path. If the average is 621960 hours of life, then caring for the only vessel that is provided, no matter the current damage, makes sense. Doing what one knows to be the most outpouring head held up high possibilities. To be proud of 621960 hours. To spark the internal fountain, to put into it what it needs for it to release all that is and was meant to be.

# Swans Of Purity

This shared celebration derives from my true newfound awareness.

    Life changes. Something happens and then we are not impervious to finding ourselves in the valley of uggh. There are lots of instructions of how to delight in inner peace but somehow the roadmap of how to get there is distorted by reality and other things take over the gaps and scars from life. There are innumerable methods that fill this gap and launching pad. Some are lifestyles or poisons that are
dangerous. Other things are not dangerous but are not positive.

A general old school rule is too much of anything is bad for you.

I could have been addicted to sex. That would have been interesting right! Ohh baby I need you, I need more! But, yeah right, no.

I could address all the titles that I maintain in my life, some come and go, and some are just the essence of who I am. Mother…, one of the core essence of who I am and will always be. Another one of my titles that will go is … hoarder.

    It was not intentional. It was as follows; I was thrivingly employed. My heels clicked with firm silence of authority and placement in my every step. I enthused in the exhaustive overtime and all the side purposes that I involved in. Then, just as the seasons change with golden sun and red fire leaves or ballet of snowflakes, so did the change in the flow of life.

Who accepts despair and thinks that is what they are doing? In some days just surviving and breathing can be a strong feat. It is knowing that you are worth so much more than that day instead of living only in a cycle of those days. There are some that no matter how many times they have been knocked down from the mountain, they find another way up. They live and breathe inspiration. There are others that individuals that surround them or life sings a thunder that defeats them. It's not saying that someone is bedbound and giving up. It is just saying that the spirit drags or goes numb in ways that cannot be healed in one sunset of beauty.

My employment altered and then changed. My health changed. Surgery after surgery, life, death, and other occurrences. Nightmares unforeseen occurred. Every penny all of a sudden mattered. I began relearning how to use my bowels, how to walk, helping my child that was forced into a health situation that was not of their own. Who I was had gone and I forgot the path to the strength of those that were more than the ones that were near me. Those who had lived their lives during their time and day and I carried their DNA within me. Too much was different and foreign. Although responsibilities still reoccurring and constant as life is, the grass was no longer green where I stood and was not green where I lifted my eyes to see. I could not say that nothing stood in my way for it felt like the weight of the world was upon my shoulders and everything stood in my way. I needed everything to appear as if it were normal, so I shared only occasionally what little pieces of what was the entire devastating picture. Most just wanted to know, or know enough to decide a band aid option, but that left my children vulnerable.

I held on. I held onto everything memorable. I held onto everything valuable. I held onto what I desired to be once more that I could no longer afford. I held onto things that were just stuffed into an attic from long before that now needed to service the children. I shopped at places that I would not have dared entered before. I used to care passionately for homeless and downtrodden, and now it appeared that we were one step away from becoming just that. I held on when one child grew out that the next might need it, from girl or boy for girl or boy. I held onto for tomorrow for how horrifying today continued to be. It was not that I was not trying. It was that life waits for no one and there are repercussions upon the innocent, upon my children, no matter what the circumstances may be. I let them know that I was doing the best that I could and did the most that I could to remind them of better days that they had already experienced. That was not the best approach. To leave them looking at the past, hear the surrounding negativity from others, know the difference, and to not yet realize that the past will never return as the future, was not the right approach. I could not ask them to appreciate what I did not appreciate. We held onto survival and hope of survival for tomorrow. There were lots of things the children had to stop doing. Only with answers of tomorrow with hopelessness facing today. I held on to the toys and items in the house that I had paid fifteen years into and now I could not. I did not downsize, rather, I squeezed every corner, shelf, or cabinet very creatively with every left-over item and with hope. They utilized the items. It was not a mausoleum. Life still moved, but I was suddenly a forgotten Eli Bridge bench on a ferris wheel. No matter how broken that sedentary carnival revolving ride seat may be, my children depended upon that seat every day, every cycle that life had to offer. I pushed and fought although from the outside it may have looked like I tried little when reality was that I was giving it all that I got. I should have taken precise steps and measures in each day but often the knowledge of what should be or the overwhelming knowledge of what was, was exasperating and exhausting. Doing momentary interludes was what I used to could do for lunch and now it took all that I was. Not realizing that it was okay that I was changed and approach this elephant one bite at a time, was a mistake. Not knowing where to begin taking those bites and not even knowing where to ask for help on such a humungous layered circumstance was also a problem. If the children were depending upon my strength and my strength was broken, if the schools demanded this strength, and all other financial obligations, but the strength was truly broken, then who do I ask to agree with me and to hold my hand? Is that too much to ask of anyone when everyone knew my prior work and strength as they still referred to me as "Nakita, the lioness, and Mrs. Smith". Even the best friend, as they saw the task ahead, bailed and reappeared after all was completed. It did not make them any less of a best friend. It reminded that one cannot place expectations upon another, no matter how much is thought to be, that the other cannot accept at that point in time. I cannot look at them any less if that reality was too much for them. I will not be "Nakita, Mrs. Smith" again. I have gently found a glowing new path that I am excited to learn and get to know. I have found a love in letting go, and a reminder of all the levels of helping others and that includes growth as branches upward and purely letting go. This could apply to those who drink, smoke, vape, shop, or do anything in excess. It is wired into the very fabric of one's being. It is fulfilling a part that is absent, a part that can be healthier today. Of course, this is not of one that hates or holds contemptment for one's self. But, there is something that is not healed or that is so different, to begin living again cannot happen if that part of life remains open.

# The Shell: Protective Of Life, Love, And Self-Actualization

It may take time for the scar to form. But now that mine has formed, I am happy to walk with my shoes off in the grass and feel the laughter. I feel it necessary to go to a trail and connect with nature as well as connect with the animals that the family enjoys. We have chosen our charities for our time and efforts, and most of all, are relearning our inner strength and love which renders an outpouring that is happily shared with life. We have so far to go but dancing in the beaming of the here and now. In that dance, if we fall, of course I will reach my hand out for one of my children to pick up, but for the most part they have to find their inner strength to stand and their belief in themselves just as I have to use these tattered wings to still fly. Now that they have holes in them, now that they have scars, they actually soar so much better. It may not be majestically, but I appreciate to be able to still soar so much more and that seems to make the flight so much sweeter. It is one I only desire to share with others.

Reality danced intertwining with my uncertain qualms. There were two occasions where the children outgrew shoes and I had no idea where their next shoes would be coming from. One of the children's feet is of a size that there was no way I could even begin to try to find it on a traditional on sale or cheaper methods. There is no way that I would have fathomed this from the beginning. I could not see that it was too many random items though I did know our daily lives did not equate. I spent time labeling the boxes of things that the older children grew out of.

Then, I called myself letting go. I still saw that I could sell so many things at children's clothing sales for a few bits of change if they did sell, that I let very little go compared to what I had left. It was a lot of work for what I did let go. Life is so precious and there is so many hours in a day that it was exhausting to do it all. The owner of the home then passed. I rented this place from the owner's family. Such a precious family. The owner had a reverse mortgage and all of a sudden, I had to face getting into a new place with no money, the loss of someone special, and the confrontation of me and the things that I had accumulated. You would think that it would be easy to let go. Couches twice as old as me, china, but that was not the hardest. Someone set me down and said, the children look like they are dressing in old clothes. This is devastating. Yes, sometimes they were mis sized according to season or available sizes, and I tried to buy what was in-between. They were never stained or anything with holes. I always took pictures of them. I told them how loved and beautiful they were even if they could not see it. I never had childhood photos around, so I made sure that they did. Apparently, under these circumstances, this took on a new meaning. Their history and heritage were something new that we were readdressing but I hoped it meant something more to them than what they were about to lose.

The advisor said that I kept refilling the hole, the distress, from my past that I did not allow room for the future. And the past that I was holding onto would cost more financially that I could afford, in addition to how it made my children feel. If there are times that you do not know where their shoes are coming from, the thought of letting go of years of sizes for the children, of things that I enjoyed, of classy items that can cost in the right market, it just felt like letting go of it all. They said I still held onto more than they anticipated which they thought would be a little more than a car load, but I did see. I saw the burn pile. I saw the entire back yard, at one point, covered with things. That eventually was a large mound at the end of the road. To me, it also was the money that I had planned to make which meant I could not make money selling what the kids had grown out of any longer. It was a hard thing to do when you count the time and effort that goes into that versus the possible return. Even the lady who ran one of the shops told me it is mostly people who just need to get rid of things. Another lady offered for me to buy her shop when she saw me so much and she was retiring soon. She did not realize how broke I really was and that it was like offering crack to an ex crack addict.

I also looked at the precious souls that tirelessly helped me. The trinkets of gratitude shared with some was not comparable to the help that they gave. I was plundered. Some took things without asking. They probably felt that I would never notice. It is the largest mistake to think that it does not matter because there is so much to choose from. It was a daunting process. What was moved, some was broken and just thrown in during the process. If others thought our things were valuable, even for us, they would not have done that. It would take months just to get through that. It took so much to pack it up the first time. In the meantime, the children have to figure out clothes and socks or coats to wear during the winter. It was daunting. The thought that the most valued items were plundered on top of all of this was really suffocating. But learned is also value is in the eye of the beholder. Many will walk into another's space of life and see only what these items mean from their perspective. Some, live in a very useful and space flowing manner. Others, may not. And then when you add the extreme before a dangerous level, just compact, it was a bit much for everyone that saw it. It was not dirty nor nasty. It was just a lot and a lot of decades covered in one space. I will never forget the hearts of those souls that put their bodies, their physical selves, and for some, their hearts into what they approached.

I talked with someone who cared. They were frustrated with their mother doing the same thing. We discussed how this entered into my life. How many ladies in my life, and one single elder man that I once knew of, all had begun accumulation habits on different levels. They all had larger homes, so it was not recognized until much later. One lady worked excessively but kept her trunk of her car overloaded as she worked. When she retired, her mother that she cared for had already passed. She began to have dementia. She would shop and bring it home and forget. The rooms began to overflow with things with tags on it. The mother had collected glass jars for food storage because she grew up during the great depression. She collected this even though she lived on a large farm in a decent size loving home. The gentleman had lost his wife early into his son's life. He raised his son and as his son became an adult, he bought his son a company. He found himself alone. He was highly functioning and not missing a beat by far. He began ordering items from television infomercials. They all just sat in rooms around the home. Some were never opened even at the time of his death. He passed of pancreatic cancer. When he discovered that he had it, they told him they could help him. He refused to return to the doctor and accepted his fate. Because his mother had passed of a brain tumor, this decision devastated his son and was not ever accepted by the son. None of these people nor myself lived in a nasty way. It was not piled dangerously high or obviously where things should be questioned. Yes, clothes may not be found for being packed too tightly or because one of the persons mentioned was brilliant, hardworking, yet later developed dementia. All the persons mentioned were all high functioning, on passionate overdrive. As a matter of fact, I might have been less functioning than all of them seeing as the mother that collected jars was high functioning until she was forced to slow down in her last days. What are you to do when the meaning to your life has grown up and is successful, but you are all alone? Or just simply is no longer the option? I am sure there is a list that everyone could say but could anything on that list turn just as bad as this? When you touch an item, that item had a purpose when you got it, so of course it still has a possible purpose now. It also fills a hole. Mine, necessity and fear. My past was a part of my present so how could I not bomb shelter prepare for the future. I had to release. I had to know that change was better than staying where I was. Not the location. That changed location was going to be worse before it got better and a whole lot for any child to adjust to and understand. To ask for your child to suddenly have vision and strength beyond the everyday needs after already struggling, is a bit much. The place we went to was over 100 years old, small, drafty, and in the middle of winter. We were lectured by the gas company to know better than to need heat in the middle of winter and they were in no rush. Many things were broken, some things were taken, in the middle of moving. To choose to release things is one thing. Some of those things found their way to second purposes from thrift stores that came out or the metal scrap guy that came out and gathered what he desired. To see things taken that matter and you know you cannot replace them, feels violating. It felt more violating when some of those things belonged to the children. A few of the things destroyed without feeling belonged to some that were close to myself and had passed on. There will be no replacing that. All of a sudden finding a bowl was a big deal and the stove did not work anywhere near what reality would call safe but at least it was a place, not yet a full dump but definitely needed a little help, and still somewhat safe because it was so far out.

# Lyrical Art, Oceans, Boat Rides, And Inspiration

I had to make a change. I had to make now powerful again, but this go 'round not through just me. Through my scars. People see damage from life as something inappropriate. Why not rewrite which direction of reality that I paddle my boat for. I choose to feel life. To see the color in the leaves again. But that means I must feel the truth of this and the pain also. That means I must help my children harder since I had no idea when releasing how I was going to do that.

Many exercise videos will say if you cannot do the extreme normal version, here is a modified version just for you, even yoga. The irony is that the hardest part is actually getting off of the couch and doing the video in the first place. To push past what would be the natural inhibitors in order to just try. Every day that I acknowledge that I had a problem, that I too am a version of hoarding, is me getting off of the couch. Every day that I try and stop this problem and any other comforting addictive behavior with my children, is me putting in the video. Every day that I make a conscious list of what to accomplish, what I am going into the store for, and what I cannot do (yes on a written list), then I have stood up and said I am ready to try. Yet, I still have not taken a true step or bend of exercising. I have listened to my children and how this has impacted them. You ever want to hear reality, have a child describe it freely. Even though they may have had a warm meal, if you have given up, they feel despair. If you don't believe in tomorrow and have packed away for it with examples of the past, this belief overpowers any good memory. They slowly stop believing in themselves. This is all a small portion of what this has done. I was fighting for the gasoline to get them to and from school. The schools were located far, and I knew they needed to be safe. For the car to function. For them to feel special on the weekends. For them to acknowledge those even more less fortunate than us during random moments but especially the holidays. These were things that we addressed daily. I never thought about preparing while still having moment by moment matters to be firm life setting issues but in a blink of an eye it was always a major issue. I thought I was accomplishing so much and yet there was so far to go. Even though the truth was there, how much can you explain away.

The fear will always remain. The money could return, and I could life safely in a decent home with retirement planned for all. Recall the older mother who had lived through the great depression? Her daughter took half of her jars, which took up a great bit of the beautiful galley kitchen, to the end of the extensive driveway for trash. That elderly lady very angrily went down there and got them. As she sterilized them and put them right back up and reminded her daughter who is who, she informed me what it was like to live through something like that. She told it to me through great vivid details of memory and explanation. Her family had already done well. They would not starve again in her lifetime. She wore elegant clothes well maintained for decades at a time. She did not have to do that. She chose to. Even though the closets were full, she made sure that it did not get replaced unless absolutely necessary. This fight is similar. The wiring was changed when the scars were created.

I have heard of so many scars. Things that we lose our breath to hear. Things of those who survived such as a young man who was raised in an elite household, but the elite figure was assaulting him in every way possible in the same steps as he was leading a community. Things of a woman who gained a bi-polar male grandchild who committed suicide a year or so after she had gotten him. The mother who had invested so much into her son had other children and a husband but felt the loss, also committed suicide. One of the other children left looking for love since their mother committed suicide and they did not feel like enough for their mother to decide to stay. They came back with a child and lives under family anger because the child exists. They are now depressed and feels the weight of the family anger. The family does not realize how close they feel to a third repeat. It is like the woman who gained a permanent disease that will terminate her life. She gained it with elite persons that will never come close to any legal system for what she had. She turned activist and married someone who knew the risks that they were taking but decided their life was enhanced by her presence and strength to accept and face her consequence. She was the most elegant and beautiful inside and out. There was a young man adopted as a trophy display but treated inhumanely. He survived his circumstances, but his scars were long and great emotionally and some physically.

There are innumerable scars and reasons for them. It is horrifying to hear when someone decides they do not want to change their path or take a step further. Their energy is destroyed. It is not to state why the scars are there or compare the depth or imprint of the old life that created them. It is not to reflect into the scars. It is to acknowledge what began the sandpit, the merry go round, the addictive behavior that balances the hole with the functioning day. It is re-finding the warmth in the sunshine. It is knowing that the race of the turtle can still be won. It is finding the deep breath after breathing shallow survival breaths that is required just for the next function and repetitive conditions or repetitive motions. It is refusing to cease and lay down. It is still healing without dying. It is doing nothing yet for growth, branching, and deep breaths.

Now to evolve to strengthen. To empower and recharge the life force and be proud of survival. To know what has drained, to know the history, but reach for the possibilities stronger and through a fierceness on a level that accepts solar warmth as a battle ground. It will not be easy. Each day is a reality that many may not be able to relate but everybody on the planet understands wounds, survival, knowledge, empowerment, and love but now, self-love and a self-pride beyond the vehicle of what one does to gain funding or freedom permission to survive and interact. Through memories, emotions, thought, beliefs, accepted decisions or education is in control of setting the limitations to this limitless conscious possibility.

Why are we ashamed of our scars? Why not approach the challenge to becoming a pure mustang of the third act? Even if there were only twelve hours left to the unknown line in the sand, the finish line, why not pick up and run the rest of the race with all that is left? It may not perhaps be the fastest race, but it will be the purest, truest, and best race ever run.

# The Elegant Purity Spoken And Creatively Unspoken From The Heart

We spent two weeks in an abode of a kind and most compassionate someone else. The wonderous cottage feel to their small abode made the obviously loved location feel expansive and unending. I awoke one morning to see the light glimmer onto the golden leaves of the trees that flooded the back yard. The water pressure trickled for the warm shower but everything wrong was exactly perfect. People have said before it is always in the point of view. Yet, if a mother no longer has anyone to accommodate, or an onset of occurrences renders one where fear is reality, or a daughter has retired from her main focus of life and the person she cared for at home is now gone, then it is not just a point of view. Does it just jump to the most perfect just because the things are moved around or gone? Of course not. That is like asking someone who is addicted to Oxy if they can function without feeling something in their body even two years later. The wiring is different even from the moment from occurrence. When someone looks at something and says do you not want to just live like that. I did! I was immaculate but, yet I collected. It was when the world exploded but everything still had a place. It was not everywhere. Except in the vehicle. Everyone has that room. I have a very long ride four times a day. The car was that room. As organized consumed as everything else was, the automobile remained cluttered during this period. It was not like that before and is not now. It remained that way in truth because it was how others made me feel, reminded me over and over, of how they felt once the closets were emptied, once under the bed was revealed, the garage, the silo's, and so on. Think about how many socks one drawer can hold. Now, multiply that according to multiple children and maybe a box extra just for socks, all socks, and now empty all of that at once. Think of how many socks you would have just off of that. It would have been up, but it would have been an overload at the same time and especially when they are all dumped together. That is just a drawer. That is not the entire house and everything. They are being truthful and sometimes they may even think that they are helping. But, the repercussions are that until everything returns into balance, the pain seems to overflow into the easiest dump room, the vehicle. It is a smoker on nicotine gum and patches. It is a dieter on weight watchers. It is a step that may or may not help but has manifested in that way. This is just me, this is my reflection and experience. Everything on exposure and under the microscope of all. The vehicle was on the wavelength of reflection of how that felt yet it beamed with the exact problem of excess and overflow. It does not now. It will always be an area of heightened awareness sunken into awareness.

Wounds heal. Time provides that. They teach lessons that often people decide not to repeat on purpose or they decide to approach the occurrence differently next time, definitely with more wisdom. Scars however, scars may take a lifetime to fade just some. Scars can be a badge of pride but often are not. Many decide to ignore to presence of the scars. On occasion, to cover them up. To live attempting to fill the hole of what cannot be changed. To sustain as if the person before the scar is the most ultimate perfect level one could have reached instead of waking up, being more conscious, and reaching for the most ultimate person to come including the scars. What matters but has not been made whole. Finding true inner peace is a wonderment, a lifetime, and an amazing journey. For those who feel to hide their scars, inner peace is yet a long yet worthy journey. Yet, before moving forward, I did have to find peace beyond the embarrassment, the anger, the pain that caused the wounds in the first place, the fears, the reality. True desert quiet, sunset bearing, ocean waves cleansing peace. I had to choose each moment of now. Wake up to who I really was, remove the illusionary power, quit waling in the midst and empower the strength in the true tree. Nourish the roots, become aware, strengthen the remaining branches, and reach limitlessly enduringly upward instead of lingering in the illusion, the midst.

The past will always be a reminder, where the scar came from regardless. But why not a wiser reminder? It is not holding onto pity or hatred. It is a weight nonetheless. It is foolish to think that the past will sit in the background. It does not have to be ankle weights for each and every step of the way. Now, I was frugal and purposeful today in order to live below my means, having ensured the needs, which makes maintain the lifestyle and planning for wants or unexpected occurrences much easier.

My binge was not smoking, eating, drinking, vaping, adrenaline, or the list could go forever. My binge was safety and shopping. I could not do cyber Monday, black Friday, or a sudden 50% off flash off sale. I had to ensure that even if the store had an item priced low, that it was a home necessity within a reasonable time frame. I shopped for back to school and holidays in advance and planned instead of last minute. I was not "starved" from shopping. Now, it was planned and purposeful and not to always fill a fear. It was healthier than it had ever been. In taking charge of this life, in asserting power in my own steps, in finding love as life is I am in a paradox of proudly walking stronger and listening to the heartbeats and phenomenally incomplete simultaneously.

# Entangled Fingers Of Holding Hands: Of The Eternal Friendship and Eternal Love Of Prince Albert And Queen Victoria

As I see the color of the leaves, smell the incense intensely once again, I look forward to smiling at nothing and feeling the internal fireworks despite life, not because of it. It was the case naturally at one time. As with any other case, when life has issued beatings like a bad husband of a west wind desert sand storm, even if one does not curl up into a ball, is there enough life at that time to taste the vibrant flavors of the soup? Very few are always a little piece of leather always well put together.

I never stopped helping where I could, even with nothing. With all the things that I put out, I called churches, thrift stores, and agencies alike to hope they would place as much as they desired to a second use. The desire to help back has only re -strengthened. That journey is not everyone's. Yet in learning an internal balm of healing and not just band aids, to share that love unconditionally in further ways than just sharing what was leaving regardless, has meant so much.

To be okay with all parts of oneself and make that better. To accept the scars with the features considered pleasurable. The quirks with perfection makes the most beautiful awes. To smile knowing that what caused the scars was horrific and possibly painful or life changing but although if fallen off the horse, the horse is still there to possibly get back upon. Or, get in the boat and forget the horse! It is that scar or scars are actually a reminder of strength, a possible change but definitely survival, the strength and focus to move forward and now attempting to overcome the mountain, the workout video, the storm that still remains. That is a joyous reason to demonstrate the scars. That is a joyous reason to find sacredness in every step attempted even if staggering, and to enjoy standing in the rain of the storm.

"JaZeria!"; a joyous name in determination and cause. A worthy shout when expression is compelled, gratitude or fight overcoming. Just a word to express in utterance when the bubbles overflow from within and a holy response feels inappropriate and curses are not the visual. When the blazing red sun must still be faced but the waterfall of first goals can be seen in the far distance or a possible mist from it dances nearby.

This is to feel a purity from the inside out. To recognize what weaknesses have helped fill that hole, to complete the scar that still leave pain or just habits of understanding. To glow despite life, not because of it. To smile from the inside out, not based upon anyone else. That is not to say that having another is not a wonderful thing. To love and be loved by family, friends, children, or companion. To be appreciated at work where actual irretrievable life moments are traded in talent and presence for necessities of life, often money and accolades. These are natural needs and created parts of us. However, to stand strong in your own footstep, to be proud and comfortable before another's approval or accolades, to effervesce with understanding and appreciation of self today but definitely who you are attempting to create for tomorrow; is to begin to love one's self. To love one's self in a way that every environment is just where you are instead of who you are or how you feel about yourself, others will see that love and you will not have to say a thing. It will be as if you turned on a light color to your aura and all can see it dancing around you. This can only encourage others to love themselves and appreciate that you are wonderous within your own skin. Desire to read more? Find time, one life. Sew, sing, whatever is more of you knowing and discovering you. Share that gift with others if you would like. Everybody is somebody. To deny the scars, to be ashamed or to live in the fear and pain, is to deny you and to be ashamed of a part of the strength that you wear. Is also to deny yourself and others of all of who you fully could be! Smile!

I always express to my children, "there is always a plan b". It means, it is easy to see the barrier, but knowing the barrier is not the same as acting upon a solution. Sometimes, that is a little step within a large conglomerate of a layered matter, just accepting a piece to a large puzzle. Sometimes, it is just taking a single step because that alone is a hardship that must be repeated in order to conquer. And sometimes, it is something that you exclusively are a maestro and can conquer. Dance to no music! No reason, today is your day! Eventually, the music will play!

It is aligning yourself in finding determination within you. People can only receive from you what you reflect of you. It is not just knowing or being able to feel the past. It is also knowing where we are going. A hand hold from a supportive team member sometimes takes some time to go from just hearing to listening. It takes the internal heartbeat and change to listen. It is not that it is not desired or of disrespect. Instead of an external offense, the irritational burn that remains can be that usually more than one fire is still burning at the very time that whatever is acknowledged to be recognized, enlightened, or altered. It can be often hard to fathom sometimes that anyone else can understand. It can be very easy to know that we all have scars and have gone through something even if it is not as horrific or suffocating as your something. It is just that you were amazing enough to survive. And now can leave that cocoon into a butterfly the more that you love who you are, and who you desire to be thru all your daily courageous steps. This is a love and expectation that is not dependent upon anyone else. Our interactions place those comfortable and uncomfortable expectations. This is before ever intertwining the emotions and feelings of others and adding this into the beautiful ingredients of the cake batter mix. This is the purity that is solely and only an individual and supporting and then elevating every moment through healing reminders or renewal through the purest of loves, self-love.

# THE ONE-SIDED RELATIONSHIP

*"Of course. And both very, very uncomfortable, but THE BEST PLACE IN THE, you know, HURRICANNE IS, like, IN THE MIDDLE OF IT." - Jay-Z, Globally acclaimed visionary and entrepreneur.*

Everything up to this point is from the inside out. Enjoying today, no matter what today is, being nice to oneself and appreciating oneself because of the scars and the survival they stand for not despite them. Yet, a natural part of life is connecting with others. To intertwine with someone uniquely special that fits you just as you fit them. As the saying goes, two hearts beating as one. Ying balancing with Yang. Fundamentally, the desire and respect must be there. And it is not always as easy as saying that the scales of justice are majorly tilted in one direction without looking at if there's any other past reasons of why.

Your heart screams because you understand the dynamics of your relationship have changed, the sweet dreams shared, the gentle hopes of tomorrow, and meanings of the moments that once were, the fact that the person was held onto stated once of the dreams that included the both of you but now they could care less of dinners or dreams, and now the way they describe your relationship allows you to know that all of that will never be again. This does not define yourself love or your strength even if the pain level is grand and great.

The heart that binds or separates can give power in every beat possible. The worst manipulation is one where the heart plays with the mind and creates only a river of pain.

Love feels so safe and good whether it is solid footing of your own power, knowing the joy of your heart and yourself, or whether it is interwoven rainbows. Interwoven beyond the fantasy or expectations, from the spark of the rainbow all the way through, from cradle to grave. Dismal is everything else.

Any person outside of you can only receive from you what you reflect of you. Just as we must align ourselves, meditate, self-re-evaluations daily, utilize and recognize what we consume and what in the environment has potent elements of use or healing histories such as herbs, vitamins, and nature. We must also align, connect, and recognize within any level of relational partnership. Before being miserable about the future that has not come, and even though the foundation might not be how it might be desired, re-evaluate, and communicate. Find the strength and love for all involved to accept all that might come, might be the answer. As you breathe deeply, something new might bloom and glow through.

Communicating and caring without negativity and solution-oriented minds for a full possible flow is a beginning. Many assume that others automatically know desires and expectations equivalent to mind and feeling reader expectations. Sometimes it is evaded with what they honestly have not seen, can even recognize, therefore not even beginning to know the relevance or weight and significance within the relationship. If the inner self is not balanced or certain on desire, or the inner desire is not what the outer agreement is stated to be, the full flow will always be of choppy waters. On another consideration, it can be that even if the expectations are understood, they are not purely agreed upon, incompatible, or the path to that desire is not one that both parties care to make the same effort towards in order to maintain nor reach. Therefore, no amount of time nor amount of discussions will balance two persons being on different paths or different goals for the same relationship. It must be decided then if the path will be aligned or if it is best that one person concedes and the type of relationship that is shared, ends. Diversions, hostile counterattacks, judgmentally analytical, repetitive reflective playback of former examples, or criticism can arise during discussions that is requesting a tune-up and rebalancing of the relationship. If the decision is that this is something that unity is something that is desired, then approach with focused, uplifted, positive, in the best way with heart's knowledge of potential. Staying positively focused, completely accepting the reflections as well as hearing the opposing information, and keeping the motivation centered upon the health and wellbeing of each other as well as the relationship is the healthiest conversation in order to move forward. Even if it does not melt down in this manner, if the respect and communication is maintained for the next illuminating path of the relationship. What is unknown still lies ahead.

In the beginning its an electric freshness, an elegant intertwining dance. Promises are made. Scents and pheromones are shared that heightens the exchange. It is no longer the beginning of the path. When the path winds through experiences, expectations change, or simply repetitive boredom or exhaustion sets in. Time, space, well placed energies and attentions. Whatever the reason, the relationship might be in need of rehab by both entities or just simply be over.

Sometimes, a previous healing wound that has not yet scarred can leave an open door. An animal can smell a wound of prey from very far away. The prey might run or put up a fight but from the first moment they became a target the animal knew the prey had little chance. Sometimes, our desires, our behavior, our eyes just ooze from the not yet healed scar. It is not always what is said. Most communication is what is not said. This leads to those who may enjoy the one-sided relationship. If someone enjoys the lean of the relationship, that they really do not have to try and they get pampered, that they are not in the same emotional place that they were years ago, or simply their respect or expectations are much different, then this must be respected and acknowledged in future steps taken. Transparency, we all are influenced by biological, environmental programming and external pressures. The awareness and desire for emotional intimacy balance without conflict, fears, and a balanced level of commitment, must be matched with the same motivation.

A part of why one-sided relationships is not attempted to be fixed is because some are afraid to hear the silence. To find power in the solitude of being alone. It is not an admittance of failure. Having a stronger alternative to a weaker today might be a bitter bite at first yet a sweeter aftertaste. There should not be any unpleasantness towards the pain that tomorrow is different than today. It is just the beginning of a different path that you are capable of exploring and potentially can firmly pursue just as passionately. Even the worst past has a future. No relationship should lead to further insecurities, or the polar opposite of potentially being so self-absorbed that the relationships are only for meeting a purpose or need instead of the shared connection.

A compartmentalized relationship develops out of fear, a safety measure, or being overwhelmed. Holding back actually are more barriers to others but also in turn to yourself. Enjoy the moment instead of always only seeing the end not yet reached. Fearing the bogyman in the closet because once it looked like that could be a possibility from another closet.

Yet two parts cannot fully mold into one, reach higher levels, if never melded together. In order to have a dynamite delectable dessert, all parts must blissfully meld together. All parts must work together in harmony. A catalyst to not only personal love and growth, surrendering to listening, acceptance, and strengthening with rediscovery but also connecting with stronger blissful love with those important to you. Many explore passions as the only avenue that some have available emotionally and decide to tolerate. Emotions are possibly still under the band-aid and not only are unavailable but are linked to open pain, nowhere near a scar or beginning to heal. Wonderful and kind people that can be warriors yet decide that the possibility anything they have already confronted may manifest again leaves them interacting in a safe and most intimate or most immediate measure. When expectations arise, so does the anxiety of the connectivity that exists each time. The irony and tragedy are, as one radiantly or erotically connects, there is a piece that will always linger no matter how nonchalant it is treated or perceived. Elevating the concept of you, acknowledging the realm and borders of the current to decide as the creator to your story if your radiant liberation, enlightened uplifting, mental independence, restoration, erotic enlightenment, ongoing newly discovered determination or excitement, conversion or modification, possible collaboration, needs any limits or borders that are edged in fear.

A breath must be taken. Here, a pause. Respect of others is still respect of self. It seems barbaric to repeat yet, sometimes life is so numbing that awful or terrible acts are overlooked with excuse. A devil with a smile is still a devil and poop with an elegant flowing bow on it is still poop. Ignoring depravities that cause internal cancer cannot release any positivity that is worth ignoring the extremes. It is improbable that any self-discovery, elevated stronghold of endurance, continuous re-evaluation crafting and re-creating of yourself will be allowed to breathe freely and passion valued in such an endangered tolerance. The normal outcomes are so devastating that this breath was taken to plead as the fleeting moments of life are too precious to resoundingly ignore. Every word is for love. Love from the core to the solar. Loss of life or just loss of soul is the very opposition to love.

Looking for the variable change? It is easier to see what might be wrong that another is doing or is not doing than to notice that the one-sided relationship can also be because of our own walls or defenses that we carry every day as limitations. What are your passions? Do you feel your strength and desire to fight for wherever your personal next step may be? Have you tuned up your love of self as you approach your love within another? What is your enlightened living throughout your day as you approach your happiness, health, prosperity, and consciousness? Do you follow through to create change or address your powerful insights? Your pace, your peace, your flow, your radiance, your changes and approaches to your health, mind and body, encourages and enlightens life, relationships, erotic levels, excitement, and true bliss. This may be shared with another or it may be strength that is within and shared from solitude; not indignity of implications of being alone. Proudly claim all of you and experiences, no matter the outcome. It was worth the effort and opens to who you have become but more importantly are willing to approach and share future energy and precious future goals. What wonderful openness through positiveness may excitingly manifest and bloom!

As you are cultivating yourself, viewing the world through the glasses of positive first, releasing anxieties and negatives, do you revere and consciously cultivate the relationship in a manner that is healthy for everyone involved? A relationship is not ownership or a guarantee. A few moments of just making eye contact, being fully present, interactive, honest, respectful, meditating together, supporting each other's changes or cultivate goals, and not allowing any electronic device to become the third member in the relationship. Communication is not just words. It is not always what is said. Sometimes, it is elegantly what is not said. The shared energy is mind, soul, and body which is leaps and bounds further than words or prehistoric carnal. In fortifying self, acknowledging changes and approaching lighting those fires, the endearment is to encourage the same connection to self, connection to spiritual heart, connection to highest focus and potential, of partner, children, spouse, or whomever else is in the direct intimate relationship. What could be more valuable than that? Each day before life's demands interferes, as important as breakfast. Relationships can be filled with as much drive, desire, and potential as any other of life's offerings; as a process together.

While one decides how to cope, re-adjust the scales upon, or accept the one-sided relationship, it is finding the overwhelming joy within each of us. To be thankful despite the pile of daily smog that will always be there to overwhelm, to lift the chin up until it stays up, to erase the biggest barriers and provide the biggest burst of mental freedom because what lies ahead is always unknown and therefore not set in stone which renders possibilities as long as there is an effort to just try! To revere and consciously cultivate the steps that are within reach, fortifying what is possible while propelling forward for what is impossible. A person next to your side is not the refuge, the brick wall to barrier all of the negativity, or an assistant upon limitations. They may be a beautiful special enlightening person, that will take your thunderstorm and help headlight you, offering all sorts of smiles, encouragement, special rose petals throughout each day. But they cannot be you and can only walk near you on each path. Your feet upon the path, your song and dance, still must come from your inside bubbles. Your spirits may be so connected that when they emotionally hold you, your gratitude and trust, your soul, feels and would acknowledge the intent and comforting purpose. The strength is a sunshine that must begin within and flood outwards. An amazing limitless bright love to warm others just as much as yourself. It is to be shared as we control our end and cannot control anything after we release it into the atmosphere. It is sometimes hard to wake up and just smile. However, if we know that the pouring rain is a cleanser that will help the seeds that we have planted flourish. All we must do is acknowledge the bright side even though it is easier to notice the pain. A tiny papercut is easier to acknowledge ten times before ever seeing the functional arm that is still there and will remain. To venture into internal power which will firecracker spark growth for as long as the heart is determined to smile even when it is a stretch to reason why. That smile is a spark to love from its very source. Today is the best day to want to fly, find the sunshine, and just take one smile into the next direction, no matter what comes, the authenticity cannot be beat!

It caused pause when I was once told in passing, "The worst feeling to me in life is to love someone and they say they love you too, but their actions don't show it, it makes me feel more alone then when I was actually physically alone". The young lady who said this was adopted from a horrible situation. She fought all of her life to be accepted. Accepted by friends, by family, and by those she decided to be intimate with. She thought her heart was open because she unmasked verbally her past, yet she rarely could unmask her full heart. She held her power strongly yet separately from her heart. Love comes in all forms. But when we are born, no matter how strong or weak, our clean slates already trust, ourselves and others without hesitations, love without knowing the word, an instinctive dedication and Hachi loyalty. Looking on the bright side of life, having to learn and push everything in order to function and do it with giggles as if every baby knows that they are not chasing miracles, they are the miracle.

Your mind and heart, when properly functioning, like a fine-tuned engine, are intimate organs that deeply tenderly connect that cannot be touched from the outside. They are amazing organs and not one finger can lay a touch. It can lead to limitless ecstasy and joy or knowledge, growth, and possible wounds. Even though the foundation is to encourage to stand in the knowledge, growth, relief, and passions. There is no eclipsing that Words are powerful. Words can overshadow any emotion. Words can control any actions. Words can light a passion or lock it down with flames. Words can restart a flame, create a wind that can breeze you there while alluding and evading any trees that may be in the path of the new flight to eternity of ecstasy. I would rather be touched by words that linger in the spirit than by emptiness, by intentional pain, by remnants of nothing. If that touch is shared, I will pass on making that memory prevalent to tomorrow. That dust shall not outline my form, my dignity, my powerful steps not yet created. I will not fall back into any passing snake pit intentionally. My weariness shall pass as the weight of the boots I carry do not stop me for reaching the stars, just a heavier step through the mist. I can see my goal as they twinkle at me. As I look up, I realize that they are also reflecting my brightness, through the cold darkness that surrounds us, right back at me, leading my way.

# *Constellation*

## Goodbye

*This letter was written for the intention to say goodbye. Yet, the love that it was intended for rebound their love and shed the separative issues as a snake must. This met these two lovers anew and they are ongoing brightly to this day. She was ready in her love and in her pain to let go of the one that deserved the same happiness that she sought. In being willing to release he was willing to hold on and it had the beginning, not ending, that they were both looking for. All that they approach now, they approach explosively together with optimism in tomorrow as yesterday fades into the past.*

Ase, I have tried to discuss things with you. Your responses are less than pleasant considering all encompassed. There has been collaboration with you and influence from you unmatched. The things I spoke to you on are simple. They are basic matters of respect whey you know another holds that space, no matter how simple or vast that space may be. You do not choose to reassure me or encourage in a positive light. It appears that you need me to step aside. I do not feel adequate for this portion of interactions. Yet you have watered and refreshed our flower. It has bloomed with roots that extend year after year. We will cross you positively in our remembrances and our dreams as your roots are intertwined throughout our hearts and very breaths.

Your light will continue to flourish, and we can only wish you well as our paths Velcro painfully rip apart. You will wow beyond even your own expectations as you have not fully accepted the depth and the strength that you achieve and amaze from within yourself. It is stagnating and unhealthy in this swamp that we have landed in and I wish a sinkhole for no one which is obvious if we fester here much longer.

Feel free to go by the school and see the little one as much as you would like. Other arrangements can be made as we begin to figure this out. We will honor the outstanding commitments and please do not forget about big girl's surgery pending soon.

At this point, I am not trying to make this what it is not but be and remain secure within what it is. That was not approachable and you assuming to remove one healthy portion balances another unhealthy portion just vaguely advises me to back off (an arm's length, not to back away). Yet, in this case, without communication it is the same rapids cliff approaching for the same pending result.

You are simply an amazing human being. The time we have shared will remain a wonderment in our hearts, bittersweet. You will conquer all that you pursue. Your vision and sight of all things are extraordinary, and you can only build upon this year. When the children take the trip that was planned, no doubt they will think of you and ask of you. You have truly touched our spirits as a family. You flooded our future passions.

I cannot understand the need for fluidity although I understand that all of this branches from pain that will not subside any time soon as it has always been there. Curiosity killed the cat as it is truly choking out us. Beyond the resurfacing of your geyser of buried pasts and recent matters, you will be thoroughly missed and always loved and appreciated. You are true to state that pain will cause pain and that is what has rung true here. Although the fluidity and other locked areas are of a path I will not intrude nor expose the children to the sideline of that roller-coaster, words also deeply cannot express how infinitely rooted you will always flow through our veins and rooted with our spirits. I do not desire to say this, yet I must. My soul pulls in a completely different way. From our sessions, I know you are aware of this. But you appear to need to be unbound from any expectations and standards and as hard as it will be, I will be the last to stand in your way. Beside you, I will always remember fondly. Behind you, I cannot remain although it has been my place as of late. It feels as if it is underneath your shoe. You won't hear me, but I will always relentlessly be in your cheering section!

Don't forget to love YOU. You love what you do very passionately and have others around you that demand you always. Don't forget to slow down sometimes and capture life, just smelling the roses, just a glimpse sometimes isn't enough. Don't forget that it's your life and your destiny. There's only so many hours granted to the untold end. Whatever is priority to you seems to be so prevalent that I do not desire to ever see you on rush to take a peek at that untold end. I hope you breathe deeply just a moment more, enjoying your mother, your siblings, the children, and especially you.

And know, it's because I understand but, yet I cannot. No different choice is perceived that I must leave you. You need to be who you desire to be and how. But we will always linger in the breeze that brushes by you and it will carry the breath of our love for you, respect for you, and regardless, always will. All of our time together, this too is your awareness.

## Enjoy Your Smile

The smile comes in purity, laughter, and confidence
It is a disrobing elegant experience
It is the filling overflow from a warm doughnut
A warm heart beaming and momentarily exposed
Those who crave sugar yet just guard it
Those who spread it thin like a cake in the wrong pan
Never coming close to fully tasting
Never knowing the delectable delicacies that they hold
Never caring more than a passing thought
Never able to fulfill if not to just being determined to just be okay, to just enjoy each delectable
moment for what it is instead of what it is not
The cake would have been enjoyed in the right pan instead of a thin dry spread
The fillings would have
Cherry jubilee over flowed
Bursting with scrumptious dancing impossibilities
Some prefer To lick the icing
Knowing they can taste all that they crave

To lick the icing
Discovering and tasting the deep penetrating sensuous flavors
To seek and play in laughter beyond any skepticism or fear
The enjoyment still lingering upon your tongue
A desire to ask or to say
But why
Has that not all been
Revealed within my view before today
Pained from an old black and white view
Desiring only simply the real purely suited ingredients
The ones that will melt into your hands
Are only from purity
You are satisfied
Simultaneous, free from imitations and locked down limitations
Simply, life on Smile
Life breathing knowing that the smile is with us every step of the way


(-*G. Meridian Paris*)

# Labels Like Handcuffs

Work it off, work it off, work it off
No more labels that's enough
Labels are diseases that make me cough
Labels are things that need to be doffed
Seeing labels make me scoff
If you're masked by a label just check it off,
Cut it off, drop it off, let it fall off, kick it off,
Knock it off, lay it off, lift it off, take it off,
Turn it off,
I'm not skinny, I still get buff
I'm not soft I still get tough
I'm not ugly, I'm a diamond in the rough
I won't be concealed by labels
Labels like handcuffs
Labels won't define me
I forever stay free
Swat those labels like a flee
Squash those labels like a pea
Labels on me… I won't agree
Let labels decay like an ash tree
Watch out labels, I stay beastly
Got rid of my label like a divorcee
No labels don't mean nobody
Just you're not seeing reality
Labels shouldn't define you like caller id

Labels are like diseases… can't you see
Irritating and futile like your enemy
Labels? What do they mean?
Do I need to be titled in order to be seen?
People have been labeled since the beginning of time
Treating it like no big deal… like a victimless crime

The truth is labels are nooses
Attaching to us… a play of abuse and
Enough with labels… flag of truce
Listen
Feel the tension
Of frisson
That I mention
Of this ricin
Labels are the friction
That is hidden
They're hittin'
Every minute
Of your livin'
They're your prison
That has you stiffin', trippin',
Blind to their vision
other's opinion
Of your position
Cause abolition
They're ammunition
Of competition

Not your definition
Not your recognition
Just superstition
Got me pissed and

I don't see labels
I see humans that are stable
Humans can hurt… but I'm singing lyrics of the labels betrayal
Stop holding on to labels… like a baby in a cradle


**(Corbin Leamon)**

# Ahcaz Inside Out

As the alarm sings bleep...bleep...bleep,
We wake up once more traumatized by the trifling, trivial, trite yet tremendous wall.
We ate 2-month-old Dolma and Kofta so old and spicy it was like a fiery rock fiercely
dancing La Bayadere on the tip of my taste buds.
This time a year ago I was a proud Kurd.
Gracefully singing to the entertainment of carpet weaving on Nowruz...
Before my life was a devil's blanket squeezed and as its turned getting harder and harder
to breathe.
I am burning from inside out, but I will fight until I rise again.
Consider this my inside yet I will explode and not wallow in this state.

*(Corbin Leamon)*

# Round 2

Bang...life punched me through the heart harder than the late Ali on Sugar Ray.

Compared to this experience, America is the gates of heaven.

Ever since my journey to this marvelous country,

I have learned a lot...I have fallen to the feet of earth where there was no savior.

Now I have America to comfort me as I make my way back again

I went from Kurd to American...

From lightless to songs of grace...

Now I see beautiful New Years in every home...

Eating up to date dolma and kofta on giving thanks day...

With my twisted life, I was nothing but a physical face with years of sorrow and pain behind it.

It is correct I got knocked down with the hardest hit of eternity...but America has taught me to build myself up again and make a comeback.

So, ding...ding...ding, consider this round two.


*(Corbin Leamon)*

# Claddagh-Synergy

This step. Now the focus is intentional. Each method purposeful. Each day pushed with intent and appreciated in accomplishment even more. The floodgates have opened with no desire to close. Knowing, utilizing, enhancing, encouraging, and appreciating who I am while seeing the green in the grass that I am standing on instead of always projecting into grasses not yet had.

I face the world whether it is kind in facing me back. Standing in the shadow of fear, facing the sun, realizing that no matter what the backdrop or backstory, no matter how much confidence and hope had been shattered, as long as a little drip remained, I could storm strong with a new force.

My heart fluttered in enlightenment and driving myself changing my adaptations beyond what habit told me. The sweetness of standing in the bloom of not accepting the changes as defeat now led me to the appreciation of each possibility. There was a point where just taking a breath seemed to be a balancing moment in the day. Even if someone had said this enchanting antidote was an existing ambrosia, I think according to Maslow's hierarchy of needs theory which emphasizes the needs that motivate people, the primitive level of meeting basic needs first; I would not have been able to fully find my way to this secret fountain of youth until time unfolded its possibilities during healing.

There are people that have crossed my path that their essence has left lingering long-lasting impressions as I hope I do to others along the way. One, we have intertwined our essence, therefore luminating an eternal bond, no matter where our paths may lead. Although he twinkles in his eyes from his soul when he looks through me, he is so much more than the surface. He has more courage towards his steps and stoic power with strength carried in his smile although he is a driven and focused person. I had to bloom into knowing how to love me as the me exists now, and that made room into accepting his situations, circumstances, and then whatever the outcome of what we were did not suspend who I was. Loving me allowing me to love you. LOVE intertwines outward appreciation with inter-appreciation.

This uniqe beam also shares a special light that holds him, a special bonding and appreciation. He is unique and lovely. He does not look at his expansive wings or scars. He does not look for the reflection of the beauty of his talents within the difference that is made within the lives that he touches through inspiration. Although he shelters his woes, he does not live in them. He allows others to have their choice of doing this because everyone must process. Yet, we find a passion and soft spot for those who are desolate in their woes and trying to find a fight and focus towards out and upward.

Learning the inner drive, passions, and dedication to believed focused visions in reaching our best selves and best communities has proven to be a daily reminder for us both.

In applying this and other beliefs or initiatives, no matter how meek the day may reflect, we find a smile each day no matter how meager or a laugh that may lead into a roar. A smile reflected just from being in the moment. In a moment that can only be filled by you, to flow from a spark, a gift. You are the best one who can share love and be love in your own unique way. Each unique way is a bright sun drop to enjoying today instead of holding my breath to waiting until tomorrow to match any dream or vision although still striving forward.

Jada Pinkett Smith and husband Will Smith acknowledge that they are "life partners" instead of being "married." "I needed… to see Will outside of husband and see him as a human being." "We have all these expectations," "Will comes on the show for two episodes, and we talk about redefining our relationship, going from calling ourselves married to becoming life partners," "I felt like there was a way to speak about that that was open and transparent. But there are still aspects that are private!", a wonderful life elevating quote of Mrs. Jada Pinkett Smith.

The gentleman that supports my rebirth already twinkled in his eye when I was as slow as a tortoise, but he also supported and encouraged me not to settle for my least. We discussed our balance, and how we are individuals of ying and yang first, then coinciding with each other as if it were an orb of heartbeat created from the roots of the tree of life from the center of us both. We do not sacrifice any animated part of each other. We have learned that we cannot force healing or visions for another, just appreciating their healing and continuous daily focus for moving forward instead of sedentary acceptance. There are rules of expectations established in both of our childhoods that exist within the core of our elder families and then surrounding local societies today. We have accepted that we are breaking those rules in order to positively evolve to confidently smile within the truth. We also accept that even though there were positive aspects of our past, we do not desire to be who we were. We desire to make better the person that we have survived to be and who we were bonds us in understanding who we are focused upon becoming with who we are. It is not set as an expectation, that would set another mountain to climb. It is set as a winding path to be enjoyed together, a goal. As things happen with that path, the journey is taken together. Sometimes, some are walking the same path and they decide that another path is best for them. Hopefully, they feel that each person has left the other in a better place than when they first began the walk together.

It took so long to push through pain, like undressing, knowing that I have not yet become the phenix but determined. I know what was on the last path and how much time was dedicated to it. I see that this path can be more beautiful than before. The last path is a determined reminder of pushing forward. I appreciate the strength and encouragement of the person that only sees more beauty as we each have had to heal and grow. They could have been exhausted, feeling like when either of us had a bad day that he was bearing the weight or that there are stronger, sexier, and women with paths that the earth shakes when they step and sought after them. They are within his reach. He decided to heal his wounds with me and I respectively with him. If we should decide that we are not full life partners, I am better for the time that he decided to walk my path, and hopefully he is also.

I adore his imperfections and he responds kindly to me. It was truly discovered that the areas of our deepest wounds were also the sources of our greatest impacts. At first, what was most obvious was oblivious at the same time. We know what connects us. The outer shell would reflect that we are not just connected through our scars, the background similarities, where we have been in thought, location, or culture. The white center would casually recognize the indefinite commons that we share such as cooking, the children, our visions and dreams, our untraditional life's journeys paths having merged, our spiritual depths and quests. For the lava core, the indefinite depth, he states with no limitations, "our destinies are woven together designed by powers long before us and will be there long after us. When we were woven together, even though we were great individuals, combined we enhance and motivate each other. It brings our powers to gasoline, which sets them ablaze. That is so much better that us alone, and that was woven long before our individual names were ever decided upon."

It begins in sharing the sheered illusion of the vision while connecting our hearts, essence, path of mind, passions and motivations today. We don't just love by physical carnal alone, with routine of life in-between. My feet knew how to dance. My heart had to learn how to. Now, we touch more than just the body, but also the heart, the soul, and reach to share the light outside ourselves where we can.

To touch inside you have to be inside. The heart is something that can only be touched by another heart. Flames of pink heartbeats to an everlasting tree.

Love is a magical sensual aphrodisiac that bursts passionately, confidently, under magical romantic curls of mountain air bursts that take different shapes and different forms. Love can be shared with others through the magnitude of small touches or the wonderment within a flood. All of this is in accepting whatever the footsteps of the past were, whatever hot coals had to be crossed, that finding self-love allows the room to love another and to move with the strength to tomorrow. The ocean of tomorrow might be vast, but it will always guide to a brighter promise as long as the load you are carrying has been lightened.

We all have a story, so shouldn't this connect us all to finding that smile, not the next item on the list but the next evolution in every individual path that is just a little more beautiful than before?

Not the fake smile that hides the 'you could not even begin to understand', that holds the secret, the wounds that would rather be protected than allowed to heal. Just as a child might wince, react, and attempt to guard the wound when something must be cleaned before the band-aid is applied.

The smile that is finding the steps that lead to your good things. Not changing the inner perspective of who you desire to be which in turn is leading and guiding who you are; but the smile that is led by the hunger within. The hunger that stands upon knowing no matter how broken and how painful the situation is, fixed may not look the same, but just like the body creates a scar, there is a way to be fixed and a way to share the power and beam of that fix with others.

We both have independently felt breaks in life where it was as if swimmingly every time we came up for air was if we were swallowing more water and sometimes straight drowning. We knew that we would dream during those times of new and far away possibilities because they were safe, exciting, pure, and no one can remove fantasies and dreams. Although dreams can communicate so much, dreams are not the same as actionable goals even if projected. Goals should exceed reality and dreams should help find your own magic that will burst confident passions into reality. No matter how bleak or broken the outside world may seem, there should be no blocker to how explosive and how uplifting one can dream.

Sometimes underneath the sunrise, the breath slows to a harsh pull in and knives floating out. Nothing denied, all raw. The unicorn does not fly where this pain lies. Yet, underneath the same sunrise is where all the hearts lie. It is possible for the rebirth, the electric shock, the determination of just one more jolt to burst anew.

Juggling so many balls, only seconds of life in-between. Only surviving in the margins or the P.S. of life. Feeling like a broken candy machine out of order yet still holding all the candy. The weight becomes heavier, as if every struggle to reach the surface, every gasp for air, is not only met with gulps of water but also sudden weights bound to the body. The frustration, how long will I be drug to hold my breath, through life?

The weight may become heavier but there comes a point where it is a painful option. Just as those first gym exercises burn, just as a gardner must sweat and hurt their hands and back to weed their garden, at the first shimmer of light, it must be dove for with all force. It may just be a crash in the dark in a reflection of a star. A processing out, purging, with a focus and enlightenment.

We determine what to weed and what beauty or hopefuls remain. We create ways to carry the weight and then to dump the burden. We find the strength to accept the consequences that we have already suffered but do not succumb or surrender to a remaining sentence. In the core we realize that it is not what meets the daily complaint. It is not what is there, it is what is missing. I cannot complain while surrendering my strength. The life we all desire begins now, right where we are, defending the impossible, and creating an impact. It matters when others do not believe in the core of a being. It matters more when the core of a being cannot quit on themselves, find their fire, utilize that blaze to the most powerful of its ability. Conquering when the fall has already been hard. Caring to rebuild from the inside out. To remoisten and reshape one's own clay that was misshapen. We walk as chameleons, but the true change occurs like a transformation into the renewal and rebirth of core essence, into butterflies. Not for greener grass. Transformation creates a fountain from opening oneself up with all current possibilities, and others, like a blooming flower. With profound endurance, unaverred by any negative smoldering of others, liberated thought, acute vision, approaching your fear with strength until there lies truth, single step by single step, can lead to any invincible possibility. Breaking in, breaking beyond the set images and circumventing the existing limitations is a love for self like no other which can only overflow into an ecstasy to be shared with others.

# Mesmerizing Gardens On A Plate And Healing Red Clay

Pavlov's theory of classical conditioning has demonstrated for us how easily one's fear and one's mind can be changed. Fear, hesitation, personal barriers, cells recalling the limitations of previous moments, repetitious behaviors, lack of adequate sleep and foods, and looking at tomorrow through the past.

**I became prepared for the moment. Then, the moment became prepared for me.**

*When I drive by these trees on a long stretch of road, next to the airport, I roll down the window and let the speaking breeze flow through. Nature has always fascinated me in unlimited ways. These trees have grown in the middle of a field with their roots intertwined and they stand together. It can be seen that they are two separate trees. Almost of the same measure and their branches are similar yet not the same. As I drive closer, the trees appear to merge and at one spot, they appear as if they could be one singular tree.*

*One view is to see the two trees and the separate entities that they are. Another view is to see the separate parts of an individual and how lovely it is when they are harmonized. Of course, in acknowledging that they are separate trees one can see that they stand strong and bright on their own even when close to another.*

Life under repair

"If you don't leap, you'll never know what it's like to fly."
— GUY FINLEY

# Productivity And No Holograms

What is the source of the pain that is carried like luggage every day? Whatever project in our lives are in the forefront, they receive lots of attention and care just as a garden would.

There are numerous methods to weed one's interior garden. It is not the method of expression that matters. It is that the internal weeding occurs leaving a clear view and a chance to move forward without caring so much in every step as a negative.

Long ago, I spoke with a gentleman at work. He was in turmoil. We spoke, and he expressed his thoughts of his recent mistakes and regrets. He sternly warned me in his infinite wisdom of his learning the value and purity of love and not waiting for greener grasses before beginning today. He knew his reasons for having been focused and one sided. His wisdom at the time was being hardnosed would have paid off. He reflected:

His overall reflection was that he felt that he found fault and did not find solutions. He thought he had given anything and everything to it, but he did not give his own time. He did not find or discover his best self, his own abilities or able to use his abilities to any potential before using his learned skills to delegate his life and therefore his path.

He continued through points:

- I should have found a way to get along with my in-laws
- I should not have rented a temporary house two months after I got separated
- I should not have let her go when we were seeing each other on that special occasion. I should have told her we could work it out.

- I should never ever have let her leave that night when she was crying and telling me how much she loved me. Not that I control her. I should have responded passionately and interactively.
- After dating for a few months, she was unhappy because she did not feel our dating was leading us anywhere. I should have shown her and described to her a future together that we both wanted. I should have made her believe and then I should have found a way. I do not know to what degree others affected my judgement. But, I was lucky to have that opportunity and I shouldn't have squandered it.
- After she told me she had met someone else and they were serious and thinking of getting engaged, I was shocked and hurt by the way she told me. I concentrated on my hurt instead of the desire to be with her. I wrote her a letter describing that hurt. Instead of doing this, I should have fought for what I wanted, I had left the scales tilted in our lingering relationship for so long that I could have just shown an effort from my heart, or just asked her for a chance and not given up.
- I was arrogant and couldn't believe she had found someone else so quickly. Surely, he was not going to be as good for her as me. I wanted her to reach out for me. And while I waited for this never to be to occur, my chance to win her back passed me by. I needed to win her back, but I did not see this.
- I was the defining factor, but I allowed everything else carry the variable.
- I should have sent her flowers, and I should have called her. I should have convinced, and I should have fought for her. But I did not and now I am the one who is paying the price.
- Years ago, when it became clear that I did not want to work in this same line of work anymore, I should have changed careers by choosing any other career. Instead, I held out until I found the perfect career and because of this arrogance. I am still in the same career and the same comfortable paycheck. I found fault with every possible career choice and therefore never found a solution.
- When we first moved here, we moved together. She wanted a Mercedes. I should have agreed and let her enjoy the experience. Instead, I was worried about money because

I did not want to stay in my career. I should have discussed this with her. I should have found something within my ability zone. I should have had faith and trusted in the future. I should have found a way to achieve her goals and my goals at the same time.

- I should have been able to find a way to buy a house and have a child and still feel able to achieve my other goals. Instead of finding fault with the idea of committing myself to a house and a child, I should have looked for a solution.

- Arrogance, a lack of faith, with horse blinders on, and impenetrable unflexible view, have robbed me of the most special gift that was given me, and I shall forever pay the price.

- It is not only too late because she moved on. It is also too late beyond the bruised and broken pieces because of earth shattering news that wrenches me.

- No matter what, a piece of my love is gone, and I have only been the remainder. I did not achieve at what mattered the most. I forgot to enjoy the sweet nectar of what I had, and then the best pleasure offered to me was gone as if love were as delicate as a floating bubble on a hot summer day.

# Cupid's Arrow Struck
# The Greek Apple

*There are insurmountable resounding connections all around us. Some can be smiles, some can agree with us, some can remind us or enhance what we already know, and some can just connect, heal, or encourage the awe for the smile. The smile that is the doorway to the love that all of us have centered deep within.*

*We have all seen it. Through all forms of living energy or created atmospheres. Although a few snapshots follow, this is not limited to local nature. It can be endless and abundant in all fragrances, energies, lives, and creations that surround each of us. It is allowing the passion to open the desire that provides for wherever each individual internally and externally might be. Your life has significance and only you know what that is or is not as you believe in yourself.*

*It is the jar full of beautiful pebbles that appears full. Then, a liquid is poured into the jar. The jar receives the only thing that would fill the space and enhance the pebbles that it was already carrying. It created a new look to be viewed upon within the jar. That new look, might be an overflow of love.*

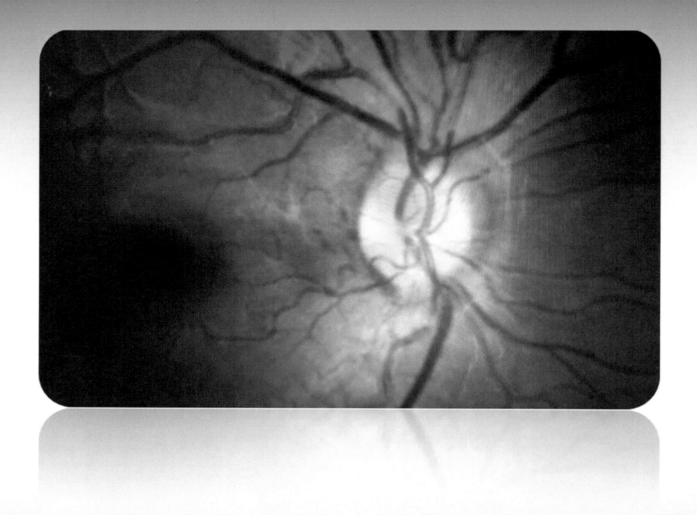

# Lace Parasols And Intense Gourmet Chocolates

In the winding path of new expressions, in finding a balance and replacement for the fear of tomorrow, enjoying today no matter how meek it may or may not be, I wrote a story for a magazine that asked for a short story. It was not the expectation of winning or being fierce out of the door. The magazine had parameters for the writing entries. It is starting where I was, it is growing my roots into a vision into emersion that did not submerge under pressure. It is embracing the difference. I set aside a few moments to declutter the outside and focused the energy into this project. The words that fell together, the simple short story, closes this short thought but also opens to all love and endless possibilities which is where this path led. The short story was as follows:

# UNITED ENDEVOURES;

## UNIFICATION IN EXTASCY

As she felt the twinges in her body she didn't know whether all of this was worth it. She knew what she was trained and built for, she knew that he had resurrected her. But was she a project or was she truly a savored gem to him? Why question it. Because right now as her toes curled and her nerves twinged, she recalled that she had pinkie swore to him in a half-naked video chat that she would not be with another or of any kind, she would not make herself cum.

When he returns, she will caress him in blessed waters in spiritual re-connection surrounded by candles that would only be for balance for the heat and mood will reunite simulating lightening painting a sky. Although she would love to just go to a store and video chat him from the dressing room to share how much she missed him. She would try on everything that he desired in sheer delight and moved in any leg caressing, folding, or popping direction and angle that he pleased. She then would take the body paints and trace his sweet breath that lingered with her onto her body, anticipating then developing a unique enjoyed sensationally pleasurable creation a design that would include lots of color and lots of delightfully waiting creases and locations all smiling for him. Everything that he enjoyed seeing would be purchased that day awaiting his return for an up-close view. Yet, it is more than his body that is missed. His smile, inspirations, and touch changes every day to a sunny or at least a possible day that promises tomorrow. The shared synergy.

As she laid back missing his very touch and reminiscing of his gentle repetitive kisses she arched her back in bittersweet excitement. He knew how to run his fingers softly and rediscover her body while showing gentle appreciation as if most moments, no matter how many years repeated, were individually indulgences of new. She thrilled in returning some of this satisfaction unto him. He knew where to kiss her that was not so obvious that matched the twinkle in his eyes when he peered through her soul and seemed to be able to dance with her there wrapped only in their aura layered colors. It was the time, the effort, and the warmth of heart. The place never mattered and could change, props or toys, the mood and circumstances would rotate, but just like the sun on a solar system, that always rotated around them. The empowerment in his voice, it was all she could out pour in reflection from her soul as she debated satisfying the simple carnal need that erupted from the very core of her base Chakra. As she began to give in and touch with a familiar rhythmic find of her own explorations, she licked her lips and moaned out only with a craving desire for his taste yet with an overwhelming feeling of cheating. She hungered like a panther to rotate her tongue upon his most gentle to his most firm. Memories of walking with him as his hand gently would explore under her dress as if it were a secret, for him to only be greeted with drips of anxious pleasure. She would have to wait and the ride in his big black truck would vibrate every location that was soon to melt to his every whispered pleasure and demand. These reminiscent thoughts only sent sensations through her nipples and made a forced waterfall ready to explode although she did not yet yield into the sensations that were created by his lingering essence. He lived more on the balanced side of life, a rhythm that included health and nature with practical expectations and experiences. She knew even if she could talk him into the thought of using a virtual reality suit, the mechanics of it still cannot add his sensuality although she would love to even just feel his hug long distance right about now. She kept going, reaching over and grabbed her toy. An explosive craving to go further but ran it along her leg as they quivered, and she knew what she would be giving up to satisfy this moment. The fight was so much harder but for purposes that were to outweigh this simple moment. Was it a practical request? He knows that he frustrates her on occasion as his time is precariously limited even when he is home. A guilty awareness flooded her as she often presses his time but desired only to open and uplift more free rose smelling ground touching moments as her soul wants to heal him as much as he had offered a path within her. She needs the distinction of his touch, the dedication of his path, and the intimacy of the fire that red and blue can create as it dances. Two souls could not be more improbable, yet it is something about the new creation when the red flame and the blue flame intertwine. It was honorable of him to want to wait until he could unite with her again and only requested that she did the same. As she ran the toy up and down her leg, closer and closer, she wondered if she could talk him into teledidonics, which can be controlled by WiFi and Bluetooth. He doesn't mind gentle skyping over the phone. If he had the remote app or one like it, connected to his and her toys, then not only could he manipulate things from long distance, but he could also feel the movements given to him by her in real time also. Yes, it still doesn't hold his essence, the unification of the souls, but the connectivity that frays just a touch during times of repetitive distance and distractions resounds the more that is put back into it in all areas to include this one.

As her common sense appealed to her libidinous aroused desires re-balanced an understanding that all of this is not a euphemism for but a symptom of the love-soaked heart and a spirit that had been ripped into two places. There was already a slight roller coaster before he left which she decided she will not fold into but took the tracks and planted them into the tranquility of tomorrow coupled with his heart and his words overall that overshadow any bumps.

The conversations over the miles are short but conveyed dripping with affirmation and honey. They feel each other's spirits and know who needs a song and who needs focus. They are each other's pillars and they rotate in the carousel rhythm as if they have their own music and direction. The dazzle, distinction, and dismay that is felt as adult or child alike as one approaches an ornate carousel for a simple few rotations of a slow appreciative disconnective reflective time of long ago; is the same feeling in watching the wind dance that are these two impossible yet kinetic interactive bound energies. They are the flying galloper horse, and all that they love are dragons, horses, unicorns, and other sun dipped animals that are there, as those that they care for would be the bench seats or cars, all realizing that this couple would fly them to a different plane if they were not mounted but they would guide them and shelter them with all their shared love and hope. For her, there was no doubt that she had to take that ride, allow him inside the barriers that she always held high, in order to stand by his side. Now, she questions if the flame that is lit, but protected under hurricane glass, if he ever desired it to burn hot and bright. She did not need to burn down a forest, but she needs the heat and there is comfort from a flame. There is eros and solitude when the camp site has plasmic controlled fire. The elegant intensities of that passionate fire also provide light to all those within its realm. She reflected of all that they have discussed and the path as it viewed to be which is not a choice but a light that is found and rediscovered often as reflections or erosions may interfere.

As a past cannot overshadow and one cannot stand in triumph overwhelming to the other, she laid back allowing her heart race and blue twinging amative frustrations to attempt to calm some although the reminiscent undertones would still definitely residually remain. Her breath still was laborious from teasing with mechanical delight absent of pleasure and enjoyment of his spirit, his very toned body; she performed the prayerful ritual. Gently directing her energies and prayers not just limited to but mostly centered upon his spirit, his wellbeing, fearing often for his safety as his footsteps never wavered, for his strength of heart and mind as he had to challenge and accomplish so much with intense continuous noise and for fluid successfulness with his focused intent for his absence. His tranquility is expansive. His focus and energy are explosive. His empowerment of others is his gift. His grandeur is equal only by his oneness and connective energy that he shares with all in a limitless desire to be a help with those that want to help themselves. His exquisiteness of being is matched by his maintenance but not over obsessiveness of form. Hair of Sampson, with the most delicious, toweringly toned, well maintained, casing of a body for such a well-rounded exquisitely smart individual. If Leonardo DeVinci had ever crossed paths with him, Leonardo's "Vitruvian Man" would have been designed after him as he picks up where that model left off. All of this is countered in his continued desire to always pin-sightedly very precisely focused with explorative realms to improve endlessly until his endeavors often will wear him thin and peering through on a daily basis is a reminder that he is human in subtle ways yet in harmony and balance of all that he is. She appreciated that these moments he does not rant and rave but collapses into her arms. He will half listen in curiosity as she will always downplay anything she is attempting to accomplish as that never needs to overshadow the few moments they had to reconvene their hearts, align their spirits, have their thoughts compatible or at least understood by each other, enjoy or relax in each other's presence. She tended to be weary and tempered if it went down that path and enjoyed him too much to remain forever in that lost space. Her new mission, to provide the fuel back to him that he provides to her. His extreme energy and his empowered stomp through life without any hesitations or hindrance balanced and intimidated while always fueling empowerment into what she was, is, and will be. She hoped and appreciated that perhaps she balanced his jet fuel neurotic determination and definite capabilities with a smile, a reminiscent grounding, a repair, before he takes off in his rocket once again. That rocket fuel is what restarted her, what pushed her inside even harder. She recalled all of the bruises from passionate eager saving others before, but it is a renewal as if she had been in a cocoon and all it took was the rock, the love, the confidence to challenge and redefine the warrior that had been hibernating. He stoked this fire, but she had to accomplish it. He has no idea the years of renewal that is in blasting undertaking during just a few months overhaul because he already loved the outer shell. He has no idea of the lightening that is about to be by his side just because he showed his vulnerability and looked at her and said, I love you, I believe in you and took the hash of not only the detox of body but then the detox of mind to follow with a wake up as if she had been frozen in an ice cube all this time.

She was placed onto a regimen that helped her approach the shell shock of leaving the past and approaching the future in a healthier yet more compounding future. Centering her Chakra did not begin to push past the pain of healing. That pain was soothed by optimism of the future; already knowing the capabilities of the past. She added exercise, and more, back to her regimen but it was not near what she used to or could do with her eyes closed. She was fighting for her children, her love, her life's work, with passions that she carried in-between.

She exercises her mind, body, and soul as she awaits his return.

"One, Two, Three, ...Thirty-One, Thirty-Two..Crap!...Fourth-Nine, Fifty, He will never regret believing in me...Fifty-Five...I need to see me for I believe in me too"... stated aloud as she burned her body muscles just into reawakening. She knew he would not see a dramatic difference but if he could just tell that she had not been sedentary, that she took his words as her spiritual job for how else this natural born warrior was to exceed his vision and to reach excitement within herself unless she fought quietly from the spirit. It brought a joy and a peace that was reawakening. She would be the warrior she once was but now not just for others, also for herself. The workouts, they were necessary. Floods of when trained persons saw her as the barrier to their property or life changing in former successful confrontations, reminisced within her as it pushed her harder and longer for the battles that lied ahead. She recalled a telephone conversation as a local pastor informed her that they had been given two homes and some apartment units. They had already relocated a woman and a child, and a young teenage boy. They did not realize what they had gotten themselves into nor that these people need help from all levels of their community, not just housing or education. It, is not to make herself into a powerhouse. She is not built for that although admires those who can maintain such strength and agility. There is a combination of experience, expectation, knowledge, and then physical ability. The opioids were prescribed but almost ruined all of this. Choosing to strengthen the core of things of where they are and return them to the best selves without the opioids was a hard fight of a separate kind. She did not choose to go onto the medications. She thought they were helping. They were not the right ones for her and the climb back has been harder than any other battle faced as this one impacted not just her but all those that depend upon her and that she relies upon also. Now that she feels the pain that lingers without the opioids it is different but plausible, and that is all the prompting that she needs to fly with fire into any new issues and battles that her unique skills and knowledge are not fearful to confront. Her confidence is not in solitude. There are others that have chosen this plight. The confidence is in the belief and support of DeJelle, and the team of people out there that knows that there is no criteria or expectations of the individual to value each human life, a second chance, one that was essentially robbed or taken from them. For each individual that is helped or recovered or recognized, there are thousands lost or placed onto a path of no return. There are hundreds that will be mentally rewired where every day remaining to their lives they will need help just to function properly chalked up to opportunity and greed.

Making so much force to a reawakening, his absence ached her. Just simple stimulating gestures such as a ring of flowers that he would weave for her head on a whim was a sunset over a mountain. They had seen their rocks and shadows but if he appreciated her Easter bunny shell, wait until what is overflowed now that the batteries have been renewed. Her education and work history were extensive and although there is a pride held there, the therapeutic and breathing core to her soul is of the warrior to help others. Currently, all her work was online. It was fine, but it was not the batteries renewed. If it were not for the rocks in the road, and his hands running through her hair with as many versions of Hallmark that he could come across, she would not have acknowledged the true soul, true passion that she not only loved to do, but was bread to do. From childhood direct female warriors that were hands on with her like Mrs. Harris, Mrs. Booth, her grandmothers, to the military school but it was the after school Asian that encompassed more training before childhood was soon to end early and focused endeavors and life's purpose was to begin. This was not a volunteer return to a career that helped others. This was recognizing who she was, what she was always meant for, how she best had served the world, and owning an essence that she had made a topical smile, a topical identity, to hide from others. This was ignoring the easy reset of repetitiveness each day. This was illuminating the ambiance of her core of bad ass not only helping others but getting others to be able to help themselves despite any taught fears from their own scars of experience. From her own recent recognized pains and setback, she recognizes the climb that she is asking those that she is helping to do, even without them able to often be able to see the skyline they are reaching for. The opiates that the doctors had prescribed her with good intentions totally changed all that she could do, perform, and impacted her judgment for herself and others. Now, she had to work for it every day and was happy to do so in physically and strategically utilizing her skills and abilities for those who feel cornered impacted by those who do not live life by the rules or value others except for the momentary value brought to themselves. Her fearlessness is now wrapped in joy of returning to fly through, blazing the impossible, helping others maintain their self-worth that they once had and must fight to maintain holding onto.

He had a day job. He was chosen to be a civilian employee to the newly created Space Force; the sixth branch of the Armed Forces. The Pentagon had extensive background on this but still creating this into reality and leaving residual efforts with the Air Force proved challenging. It had to be stipulated what branch of the Space Force would directly handle turning over top-secret discoveries and how to help Anno 2205, Musk's SpaceX, reducing satellite clutter, and believe it or not even projects such as the Seasteading Institute's floating city. His passion and driving force as a part of him is that he is a creator, a voice, a light, and also an artist. He never just creates. The purpose of the piece seems to excite and uplift even if the message may not be fully recognized and received as given. His murals are an outpouring of his own energy from a direct fireworks of lightening paintbrush that exudes of his very inner soul, often to drain and exasperate the rest of him but with the intent that a very piece of him is shared each time to uplift, and not just an exhibit of his talents. However, that piece of soul seems to reach an awakening for all those who decide to come within their paths. As time moves forward, often many will attempt to preserve or relocate the art s not to disturb the authenticity. One was painted over, and the location seems not as whole as it once was. It is a vibrant extension of him which is what makes him outstanding. It is not just a function or a duplication of an ability to demonstrate a capturing of what we encounter or visualize. It is the vessel of sharing a message with no words that is exaggerated in such curves to the belief that many will transcend time. Messages that are connective with a broader understanding, a unique reach within but also with what surrounds us and what was forgotten or often ignored due to the daily blinders of the horse race. All united through his oceanic rhythm and flow of translations easy for any language to receive. And now to reach those who will function in locations, that for the majority of us, our telescopes have only seen.

Innumerable civilians and new military cadets alike were chosen for the uplifting the new Trump branch of the military that will conquer missions of time only seen as rumors or wishes at the beginning of its birth. He has no fear, it's fitting.

He searched for her with his soul that had been drained and found her at the Earth's top. Before she was a weapon, a mother, functioning, and then broken. He loved her and now she overflowed with determination, appreciation, and no regrets. If life had brought them both uniquely to this point, she was going to never turn off the turbo that he has placed within her, return to being a warrior for others that are in traumatic situations, and always be there for the one single person that not just believed in her, but saw beauty and promise in her at her weakest and worst.

He must face his glorious destiny of being chosen to leave to create impossible imprints upon structures just now created for centuries to come. His clarity changes as the environment gives demanding for him to give back. His grounding is within her, a tattooed pale reflection within his heart as he travels. He knows effortlessly that she is thankful for him as he has promised a barrier of protection and guidance with his love, no matter what he must face or how far apart, he knows she only wish to re-energize him, uplift him, be secure within him as she goes forth also, as he is always returned to the next mission. When he is home, he is the only one that returns the same for her. He pushes her and protects her as she is there for everyone else. The missions or trainings always seem to displace him, impact his perspectives, are emotionally draining, and physically altering his bones and heart. The synergy needs no definition, regimented timeline, or demands upon expectations beyond what the heart has already created as the bond intertwined.

As he has been on this training session, it has been rough. There were anonymous letters to arrive, two together, the last after he had left for his training session. They began after it was revealed that he cheated on her and created an awareness and a self-felt insecurity. It was the bite of the fruit in the garden of Eden. There were other odd moments that would mean nothing alone but compounded once all of this seemed to fit in only months. The most recent anonymous letter stated an apology. It stated that a woman wrote it on behalf of a love-struck friend who thought his chance slipped by him. It said details that she felt a co-worker who pushed the envelope when he spoke and had the talented capabilities would have had better reason to know. The woman claimed to apologize and said she was basically misled by her compliance for her friend's heart. There was blood on a porch. This letter indicated that there was a food gift left. She had spent days in his arms and only to return home to have found that blood on that occasion. The house bordered an endlessness of nature, so it was practical if the undesired gift was hauled off by animals that would eat weekly scraps from the expansive yard. When he left, the situation held the fragility of the insecurity and the poignant punch of the anonymous letters that were not of a beautification, that were geared towards the most methodical nastiness possible. This was coupled later with a head on attack in the yard and some online methods that let them know that this was not a game but someone attempting to target her child that he emotionally adopted. Just as chilling as startling was the head on attack from the person that was around the vehicle suspected of attempting to place a high-end tracker on it. When she simply went outside after a good rain he attacked in attempting to get away. They strategized. This is what her world did best. Only, she was not used to it crossing into her private world. That is where she folded. That is where her emotions and smiles lived. That is where she could let down her guard and trust with her heart. That is where she rejuvenated. That is where she had room to cradle into him, to let him lead not only the day but her heart. Now someone has decided that a personal attack was necessary. It was one thing to help others through knowledge and experience to be able to ultimately reclaim their value to their identifications of the only life that they have been provided to live. Yes, it repetitively takes someone's income from them, but it is saving the lives that would have terminated early, provided them a second chance, but this was one time that it was threatening everything that was rare and special in her life. She came to the realization though that no matter how bad this got, his heart was either bonsai yin and yang to hers, or all that they are would be nothing more than long term motions with smiles. She knew he stood by her, he called each moment that they are together not "spent together" but an investment. She knew that no matter what caused the previous and only bump in the road, this was threatening and worse and it was her territory to handle it. As if she were a mother cat of the wild, she strategized and became protective. She meditated and centered her force. Now that she found her footing, she would protect her family panther fiercely. With her work, yes, it is personal when you impact someone's feeling of ownership. Simply though, you cannot own another. Intertwining agreements, expectations, understandings, wonderful unspokens, unfortunate manipulations, or broken forced circumstances and environments that render no choice. From the best and from the worst situations we all feel connected and can be through blood also. Yet there is only one connection that matters. It transcends distance, space, and time. That is the connections that our hearts provide. Those that have it will never abuse or misuse it. Those that value themselves will never combat another for releasing the soul of those that have been suffocated or damaged within the uncaring hold of another.

She was once told by a door watchman, who stood thick as a door himself and held the history of Europe within his voice, that he was able to drown out the screams and cries after a while. He never once had a nightmare even once that he knew that one of the younger girls internally bled to death and he held his post unrelentingly despite the cries of desperation. He felt that the childless young persons would have had a worse future and it was a small price to pay that they would get used to. He viewed their lives being changed, the abuse, the force, just as a shot in the arm that is temporarily not enjoyed for the betterment of everything else. He provided story after story of village after village in different countries or islands that they have frequented. Families stripped of lives that they once knew. Even though these people are tricked or stolen into this, and they beg to be away from it, they are fed, they can be drugged, they have a roof and showers, and if they die of a disease then it could have happened anyway. If they are sold to a family then the family can care for them in order to need them. If they are kept in sheds or other unmentionable conditions, in his eyes, it would have been worse the way they found them. Some in war, some the results of war, some by cultural expulsions, some just in the wrong place at the wrong time, and some were just open enough online to be targeted. It kept going. It just was horrifying how the money had tainted his view of the human soul. The internal scarring. The impact for generations to come of each individual that they were torturing. Why didn't they try it. Just for one day. If they thought it was so fantastic. Instead of being a luxury deamon, why not try all the innumerable variations that were required of those that just this one individual was guarding. Talon never forgot the words of this guard. He was not the only person to cross her path. Just the most sincere that was genuinely lost.

As she dusted off to being the warrior she always was, Talon reached into her wallet and pulled out a letter that she had kept from her warrior days before and still touches her soul as she is beginning again. She made agreements to boards and agencies to begin speaking again and helping to train awareness as usually employees are the first line of contact instead of Talon. Talon wore a claw bone around her neck that was believed to be a talon of a bird. The bird soars and is a precise strategist only performing what must be necessary. She loved her name as it represents her in this way. Talons are also the cards that have not been dealt. For those that she has had to scale out of windows, unlock trapped agents out of a closet that someone's anger trapped them into, retrained individuals of how to live within awareness, negotiations with those that felt they held the cards, she felt that her very name and very presence should have warned them that she held the cards remaining. The cards that should have been played in the first place instead of those who know very excellently how to cheat the game. It was her name and the unseen fire that blazes from her very interior soul that gives her permission to enter the game, hold the cards, and give them the heat that anyone else could not.

In unfolding the letter, Talon knew it was not the first person nor would it ever be the last, yet it was a person that had been warped to believe they only had one purpose. They felt bottomed out if they did not meet that purpose time and time again. They had attempted suicide twice, once landing them into the hospital. When he was in the hospital, the person that ran him tried to run interference on every question asked and had his ID to show the hospital but kept it in their own possession. No one knew that the frail young man could even speak English until they admitted him. Maddar was flamboyant to hide pain, strength to endure on and the desire to be pleasurable for the punishment and pain that had been dealt to him as a continuous alternative was all that he could see.

The first time that Maddar decided to speak to Talon, he sashayed up to her. Talon was eating in a restaurant. Maddar said, "excuse me". Talon just looked at him. "May I ask you a question", he said with a flip to his hair. He already must have known who she was but from the conversation to come she gathered that someone along the way had told him at least to talk to her. Maddar had received permission to go to church. "I tried. Both churches want to fix something that is just me. Does that mean that I am a mistake from God? Is that why I have to suffer in this type of life every day that I breathe? Am I on an instant ticket to hell?". Talon was not going to get philosophical nor religious with Maddar. Anyone could see that Maddar was tired of being an open invitation in a part of a growing epidemic. Every breath a life of heartache and pain no matter the occasional trained smile. No matter what is to be recapped, that will be inconsolable. So, Talon attempted to begin to put humpty dumpty back together again piece by piece by first asking the real questions. The statements that were made as matter of facts instead of removable challenged elements with inspiration to heal into other options of life. Talon always offers options and effective choices leading to find a chance to shine. Some, such as Maddar, needed to cocoon into a butterfly.

Much later now; Talon opened the page that had been opened numerous occasions before. Leaning back, reminiscent of how not only was Maddar's circumstances in his way but Maddar stood hard into his own way. She recalled how he met a prior client who whispered to him that her sons were worth the rescue, but for living, she had to learn how to stand onto her own two feet. She said how the main house blocked her exit from the house they lived in and now ever going back is what drives her and is her biggest fear. Maddar made a resounding change. Talon wonders about her clients from time to time. Some will relapse like a diet and that is more of what was drilled into them to know and believe is their self-worth that someone effectively had challenged every single day. Both the female client that had spoken to Maddar and Maddar had such delicate deliberate circumstances that they only had one chance to jump off the cliff they had been placed upon into the rushing waters of the unknown. They did come up bruised, but they did keep going. They had to still fight the currents that were sweeping them into different various directions, but they found that they could fight, they had the courage to leap therefore they had developed well beyond the survival and healing cocoon, they were fantastic and soaring on their own accord.

Talon read Maddar's old letter:

*I am dying to suck off another straight guy. I love to suck drunk guys sleeping or awake. I am in the mood to suck off someone. I don't want to talk or exchange names. I just want for you to lay back with your fat cock in my throat. I suck and then leave. You do nothing. I know that you love having your dick sucked on, if you want a quick private blow job then I will hopefully see you in your living room with the lights dim and your cock in your hand ready to be sucked. If you would rather walk to the basketball court and I will see you walk, maybe you will see me in my blinds ready for some guy to cum down my throat. Let me suck your dick. Nothing will be said or done again. Maddar*

A smile came across her face. Maddar had moved and had the second chance. Knowing the challenges that he faced, if he could do it then anyone that has that small loophole of light in one single moment had better be ready. Each individual is worth it. He had a hope of self-worth and the chance at strength within. He left with a desire to later meet the right guy for him where his money did not go to someone else and his acts were pleasurable.

Then, she read some of the words in the writing of the new person. The person that wanted to fracture an already pressed situation. The true fact is that it is ongoing and unless each person does a little bit, this will not end. Talon has beliefs that as we all are more aware, we will not tolerate, repetitions of the past of placing inferiority to others as we all are human beings with our most valued asset being choice and freedom.

This warrior was now evolving. Talon was defending those within her inner space as well as those who needed a helping hand and there was no way she was going to allow someone to continue to reach anyone she shared heart space with. Any person is bad enough. However, even worse, any child should not be a focus. That brought all inner spiritual talons to the surface. Any child has so much to develop and learn. They have yet to have defenses or knowledge of leadership and option of choices. Although Talon's warrior core reflected her energy, her knowledge, her essence, it created a flood of unity where there once was a wall of separation.

De Jelle once spoke with Talon and stated in confidence that the world would feel the impact of the project that he was procured to do, and those who had eyes to see would behold it. Talon reiterated in that moment, laying it all on the line, stated very clearly "I don't see you with my eyes, I see you with my heart...The only way I ask you to see me...". She knew if he looked at her with his wounded logic it comes back damaged. He has done it before. But when he closes his eyes and feels spirit to spirit, he works it like no other. He could have run knowing that she was going back to a high-risk job defying judgment. He could have run deciding that someone coming personally is too much to be a part of this unit of love and to stand in all his greatness. He could have thought that his sensual woman was returning to a path that he could understand yet not support. Instead, he pushed her and adored what he discovered her to be in each step of the process, and then pushed her some more. She was ready to Phoenix back onto the world, knowing that they would meet from time to time returning to their hidden nest. All if he did not look with his heart. He did look with his eyes before. He did feel his own pain and ignored the results of that pain but as she recognized that only to be the results of wounds closing that had to take time and no one could help him through except to remind him of the supportive love that remained steadfast for him, she recognized right when she was about to give up that he was there for her and began to close his eyes and see her with his heart also.

His first action, he took a wooden bowl and caressed her feet in oils of goddesses. It was his way. He opened something that only he could close.

As Talon was walking this path, Talon received an odd scrutinizing telephone call. Each of these calls are different than the last or the next to come. There is one similarity, the pressing time and how she can assist has already been carved out. Most of the time it is by people that are trustworthy that are specialist in their own rights. It is a unification that is melodic when in motion.

Just as Talon had begun to identify and appreciate the warrior being reawaken but for a service of two portions to life, no longer just one. De Jelle had just sent her a text filled with quoted wisdom fruit for the soul. De Jelle once told her "I know your all is a part of me but only I am all of me. You write your words upon my heart, you touch me, and you have made your mark...". He rolled eloquently in verbal dance this way. He was the only one who could appreciate her ying and quietness, stop and smell the roses, appreciation to poetry and sunrises, to his yang, his vocalism, drive, and passionate outpouring. If they were the same, it never would have been to be. People evolve, and attractions change as they have experiences and time of life increases. It is amazing the timing and intertwine of these two. Talon also realized in this received text moment of another of his many musical heartfelt sayings that helped her accept the challenge that had been just inquired of her this very premature moment. De Jelle would wear himself thin, his moods and expectations could fold in these moments, yet he would say that "it was not about what was exhibited or left out there, it was about what was left on the minds of those that are influenced." Talon is supportive with defensive yet tactful warmth and listens with her inner soul. Everyone needs an extraordinary comeback after a time of rejuvenation and this was the moment that Talon was being asked to do just that. Since De Jelle wears thin for something that he does not see to be the most important factor rather the conduit, and he shares occasionally how she is a piece of such a protected heart; then she felt the foundation and the comfort in the nest to Phoenix and rise again to reach the unreachable and win. In this Phoenix it holds his fingerprint, where she is now all of her and he is a part of the empowering marks within her soul along with the child that already holds a piece of her. It is time to make this damage disappear and arise to her capabilities with the connection in her soul to those who remain with her.

"I'm in", Talon said briefly in a confirmation call as her stomach did a dance only with her knees. It was as if she was standing on the edge of life and you knew the wrong step just dropped you. Talon drove fiercely to the drop car at a storage unit to trade her personal car for the job. Talon allowed many thoughts to reflect yet not to overflow and drown. Talon knew the energy and confidence that once was felt that was absent now, her throat on random felt an internal squeeze. The difficulty swallowing on random was an occasional residual of the medications that remained although she no longer took them. It was not just the heightening of the energy level of the situation although there was no denying that may have impacted the situation some. It just was something she had to put up with from time to time because of the meds she had taken. These small punishments did not leave her in rose colored glasses, rather smiles that it is possible to capture and utilize the recreated Phoenix that has soared to a different plane in a manner that is needed. Talon is exquisite in heels and professional office work. Yet, this is not her birth or rebirth. This is not her passion. She took the medications and will live with the quirks that remain.

As she pulled up to the lot, there it sat. The car. She gripped the steering wheel and released the last bit of nerves knowing none could apply or else her life and those in this with her would be at stake. As her feet hit the ground, the energy of each step brought a firmness that Talon was sure would return to confidence, only, not just yet. She slid into the two-seater car. At least they got her a return vehicle that she could enjoy. It was only hers for the single brilliant night, but she enjoyed the brief self-pleasure of the vehicle that someone did not forget about her.

There was someone of Talon's long ago past. He was Italian, and they could relate as he resigned the meaning to protecting structures and Talon helped with the individuals within structures. They both made things better. Beyond his elegance and pure charismatic dominance, he drove a car like he was making love. There were no rules. When he threw a car into reverse, you would hold on, but when he threw a car into third he made sure you could feel everything the car did that you could never fathom near possible. His collection of elegant cars did not come close to what he could do in vehicles that he knew could create a cream float which honestly, he could do even of vehicles that were not designed for such.

When Talon slid into the seat of that car, she gripped the wheel as if it were the beginning of a massage. Not in a sexual way, but a flashback of one who loved to live, she smiled and said, "this is for you", and streaked the car out with a birthday level of momentary happiness. The weight and seriousness of the destination came into focus. The acceptance of the preset GPS location meant no turning back. They did not need the mom, the person unified bonsai love with a good supportive energy under the sunrise, what they needed in this moment was the Phoenix Talon was ready to deliver the Phoenixed warrior.

As she arrived a call projected thought the vehicle.

"Yes", Talon said. "You understand the ramifications, the hand-off when complete?" the voice thundered throughout the vehicle from the projected speaker. "Have you been working out any or are we catching you cold?" Talon was edged. In truth, she had just begun. What she had been flowing with is like Yoga, a full stretching; nothing that even shadows what she used to do. It created an instant feeling of inadequacy. Talon said in a head hung tone, "I haven't done much. I am here. If that is a problem, it may be fatal to your use of my expertise and I can recommend a name of a very good person who used to moonlight with an excellent skill set. They may still be in the area although he traveled extensively". In this moment it did not matter what they said. This voice had made her sensitively aware. Yet, she pocketed this feeling to dissolve later. " Talon, we reached out to you because your history is proof and you are the person that will have the experience for what may arise, and the care and concern sensitive to the situation, are you in?", " Talon, are you there", "Talon, if you are having any reservations...". Talon finally responded. She often left an air of silence as her brain either played chess with what was confronting her or absorbed what was being inquired of her. "No, I'm ready." "Fabulous, thank you, your exoskeleton battle gear is waiting" the voice raved. "Just peachy...teach me how to use Stargates if we need a backup plan" Talon halfway joked. The voice chuckled. "Be reminded, you cannot discuss any details of destination nor purpose with anyone. They cannot have an inkling that you were out or for us today nor ever" the voice continued. Talon responded in great hesitation, "sir, I was going to speak about that. I am not under the same circumstances as before. I have worked many positions where the materials handled must be kept for the position only. What you are asking me to do is to defy all of those that care of my wellbeing by lying to them, which I cannot do. I must be able to at least say that I am going to work understanding that logically your fear is they will desire more details. When the bruising appears and other implications of suspect then their suspicions will be worse than the reality that I am working but I just cannot divulge specifications." There was a brief silence and then just sudden music. The voice returned, "understood, no specifics may be released at any time. This is for your safety". Talon replied, "understood". Someone was waiting outside and directed her where to park.

A female friend, raven hair, dressed as princess Leigh, grabbed Talon in a wrapped friend for life hug thanking her. Laughingly she said, "Talon your young daughter stood by my side fearlessly helping me every step of the way without being asked, I know she gets that from you". Talon could not even get out of the vehicle before being greeted with these comforting smiles. Her friend was speaking of another occasion altogether, but it was wonderful to see not just a familiar face, a friend who understands how this can go down. The thoughts behind Talon's full greeting were knowing this must be the time for this just to be, ready or not.

As she exited the vehicle they began with the very uncomfortable but extremely helpful exoskeleton. "If you will come right this way please", stated a fast-paced petite blond lady that appeared confident and possibly in her sixties. She carried a clipboard but walked as if everyone else needed gliders. "The person you are most concerned about is not a bio-design or anything, but they do have one arm and two legs replaced on very advanced levels. This was done intentionally, not because something was fully wrong with him. His name is Jahn Leevie. Jahn's arm was replaced to save his life. He became addicted as if he was collecting ink on his body. You work with us, you shouldn't have to run into suped up Jahn. He does have a forearm tat of a rebel flag with a name through it on his good arm. Remember the responsibility, the steps that they must volunteer because we do not do breaking and entering." Standardization's, Talon knew it varied from who is available and how urgent it was felt to be and whom it was thought they may catch or effect. This was not the embryo stage.

What she had to do and how it helped always changed. It was a job based on compassion, to help just because it is the right thing to do.

The story is never simple when she is needed. If they could just walk up and say "I need help" then she wouldn't be needed. Sometimes it is horrifying, but there is enough to bring the right attention and, in those cases, with the best circumstances, the right thing occurs.

The first victims that needed special assistance with her and the team were safe and secure. The super suit proved unnecessary, this time.

As she drove, elated, she arbitrarily listened to Lean On Me by Bill Withers, as it was on the radio yet it was so fitting for the moment.

Talon noticed that her clit was on horn like a loud weather notice. As she walked into the house, the song by Ed Sheeran, Thinking Out Loud, played and she just flowed into the elegant rose of the music with gentle dance. It was not of confidence nor judgment, just elation that all had gone well, and it was a moment to unwind. It was too late for the "Mommy" run, hug, and greet but Talon thanked deeply the one that she had safeguard her child. Although, in this moment, a sweet glimpse and a soft kiss of her child was reassuring. Talon was gazing at her and thought of De Jelle. She was thankful that both of them and that everyone was safe. She also knew that the rhythm of the ocean could change for De Jelle. But she was deeply connected and no matter if De Jelle one day needed to not return as he always has to go away, De Jelle had placed permanent waves back into her ocean and for that her love would understand and remain in truth with him shining or quiet. Tonight, she was strong that De Jelle's waves was in the same rhythm as hers and more importantly, he was still safe. Their vulnerability will always be a lingering concern as each time she goes out there it is to help those who have seen that one loophole of light but need help climbing through to that next moment. The misconception is that they do not have to fight if they are brought to the next moment. They have defied all odds but yet the next moment is where the fight begins. It is where they are open and raw, and anything can happen but hope and determination steers to make everything bloom to new possibilities. Life would no longer ever be carefree or naive. They could not throw the baby out with the bathwater, so most will pull up by the bootstraps, be wary of borderline actions that seem repetitive of what they have gone through and face the rest of the only life that they have yet understanding the rarity of having this sunset of a second chance. It is the neighbors, teachers, and just by chance persons that usually provide the understanding and supportive gestures that often give the encouragement and non- judgmental strength to keep moving on.

DeJelle reached out to Talon. They did this often as it was one way they kept the rhythmic flow connected between them. It was not a try, it was just natural. Sometimes sensual, sometimes informative or even just goofy. It was not for criticism, just a long-distance touch when separated that could not be broken and uplifted the moment each time.

*Grand Rising Kind Madam...*

*I'm good ma'am. Resurrected anew with acute hearing and even more imbued sight. This day is a day of revelation and rejuvenation. Thank you for all you do. Take care and receive the day...*

*What do you think about Vermeer who also had a soft sensual admiration for women as you do but most of his work acclaimed to others?*

*I like Vermeer's work, his most famous piece being The Girl With Pearl Earring with a movie of the same title out now. However, of the classics, I'm more drawn to Peter Paul Rubens and Francisco Goya. I love his awesome use of form and light.*

*How's it going*

*and no, I am not overly concerned to the point of worry*

*you never worry, I do admire that in you. But its required for the strength of who you are.*

*How was your day? I appreciate where I am with things and thank you for checking in.*

*(Quote for today)*

*you have no idea how hungry I must have been to receive that instantly... Thank you for the inspirational oatmeal*

*Hope you receive all that you desire today and then some*

*lol yet another air of shoes hit the dust, am I supposed to be receiving a sign from this possibly*

*I wish I could curl up onto that spot onto your chest, listen to you read and explore thoughts, it is a part of you that is missed, yes, I know, you don't believe in missed and have a timeline for how long you are gone for it to logically apply, but you are missed*

*perhaps I am only a figment of your imagination... a delicious delusion...a tantalizing illusion...*

*It's up to you if you are real. And especially if you desired to be real anywhere near home. But knowing what my heart aches for is not a figment. The special space was created no matter what else was swirling. You made it and is it so bad to say that you are missed for that and more? We all have fantastic fantasies but mine doesn't make spinach eggs and yours doesn't call you out on your play but fantasies are like a firecracker, can't stay lit up to the tests of reality and time. Why explain something to be special and pop my heart for missing a part of you...*

*I feel one with you, my mother, the children. In feeling one, I feel whole. Does that sound different? I feel as if we are in the same space even though we are not. Do you understand?*

*Yes, Spock, I understand that you are elevated spiritually different than we usually live so then no, because your quirks and special touches are missed and that cannot transcend time and space. It's hard to miss you knowing you cannot miss us even though it's from being in such an elevated way. Is it that you lock us out*

*because you know that you are going to return? No, that is not it. And I am horny, so I know you are not physically with me, but I feel you.*

*Great.*

*we left for reality. So, do you get to relax at all tomorrow?*

*No, actually I start earlier tomorrow with a trip and two events in the evening.*

*But between all that you were doing all and more of what you really want to do and that should uplift your spirits more than anything. I know you still have stresses weights and deadlines but while you decide to stop the ground with it, for*

*you have never slowed and always have increasingly satisfy accomplishments and craving of your soul, please take care of yourself.*

*They are adjusting one of the designs. They rejected the one that they have had me do twice now. You have seen it. It is more work than ever assumed. I am here now. It is all good.*

**The transparency. You have so much on you. Breathe, soar, and just know that true hearts share from a true place.**

**You are the artist. Not the purpose, but your thoughts of where they were taking the design is always what must flow and guide. You defy so much becoming devoted to being the channel. You also share in a vision of reaching beyond the stars.**

**Your centering is the only thing that is going to breathe life from possibility to reality. I stand strong as so sometimes you have somewhere to lean too; just as you have done for me. As you say, if you "don't think..." something is possible, stop "thinking", lol, make it happen. My wings are spread wide for you to fall into.**

**Here I come...**

**We lost power for a little while**

**So, what did you do? Mmmm.... no power, private closets, art everywhere...:)**

**:)**

*Are you reading the book?*

*If I read it, can I have the dessert :)*

*Move it closer to my center... :) Bend over baby, close to the atmosphere, up where the air is clear...*

*lol ... breathtaking electric experience that's only uniquely you...*

*Hey doll...*

*Hey tasty...*

*LOL...*

*Dear, what do you think of what I have gone back to? I mean, I know all that you are and that we are intertwined past the sun towards Sirius, but the fight itself?*

*You are now helping those who had come out of very dangerous situations by all other times. It is a special job of its own with umpteenth years of influence, preparation. Truly it was a calling, not a job. No matter who challenged you, came against her, she knew what she was doing was right.*

*The men who proudly stomped their peacock feathers because of the small size of you and the jeopardizing to their possessiveness as if their items were being edited, not real live human beings. Bruised or sprained, elated or hurting, your joy for a few moments of the day was to go home and see your child. During the day when you began to help with danger pay for those in legitimate danger, it drowned out what felt to be petty noise otherwise. Sure, drafting manuals, managing managers or doing consortium agreements were not bad in previous lines of work, but this is undeniably is your rhythm. You have to just keep working harder towards it.*

*Then there we are. The gray was so patterned that you did not see me at first. The fact that I was wounded inside for so very long made it impossible to believe that I could see you either and desired the compassion that we had to share. It would not be for a while that we would believe that we would want to heal, bloom, and be on the same journey together. Who could possibly need someone of these states? I saw the gorgeous strong blossom all her own that you would return to be. I felt the energies renewing and still finding glory within me. As the pain numbs from the past, one day, I asked you to trust me and to take my hand with your entire heart. No matter what else we have had to confront, as long as you never let go. I won't either. I will give the best of myself for the brightness in the day of others and you will utilize yourself to help give an option to others to have another day.*

*These smiles cannot relate the schoolgirl grin of my heart...*

*You forget dearest, I am there with you also, I already know...*

So, he is returning home soon. But, as she left the telephone with her heart in a flutter, a young lady called. She answered.

"Mrs. Talon?"

"Yes?"

"Dis Jenni, I was thinkin and thank you for being there and helpin me. I finally got out from under this guy and I want to help others with my story"

"That's not exactly what I do. I am glad that you feel better about how you are doing. There are several churches and groups that may love to have you to share your story."

"Yeah, I start up somethin wit one of em"

"Oh yeah, that is great"

"I've been doing good girl, I've just been workin' and workin"

"That's positive"

"I've been gittin' at it, wat you asked so I can deal but the hardest part is just to write it down"

"Well answer me something. How did you go from running to escape from a house naked, ran past people who just did not care nor desire to get involved, you ran until your legs were tired and your feet were bleeding, and they literally carried you back as you were worn out but still against your will to having the mentality and force to be able to know you can live despite the threats and challenges? It's just to reveal to you as you look back upon your own words that you have taken steps that many cannot an you can keep going if you should so desire."

"Believe it or not I thought that I was his favorite, in love with him or at least doing right when I was making him happy, but over time of him saying how worthless I was, I got to the point that I was fed up I mean really fed up. There was one time he told me to catch a ride with one of his friends. The friend got across state lines and expected what every man expected. By this point this is what all of his friends expected. His friend said I had to do his dog or not only would he not drop me off and leave me in the middle of like nowhere but he would make it bad, real bad, at home. I had to do a dog.

Then some nights he was sleep and I was up like should I kill him you know what I'm saying.

It's like you know, I'm the one you know, it reversed it."

"What do you mean?"

He felt what I was feelin'. Now he's like that towards me now, it's like switched. I can't beat or cut him or lock him in closets or laugh at trains bein' run on him or nothin' but he be askin' me to come back to him and promisin' everything but I want to stay gone. I feel better bout me girl, ya know."

"Mmmm, it sounds more like you're considering it. Why are you even talking to him? It took more than me to help you. How did you know you were strong enough to combat all that he had in place the first time that you left?"

"I had people to call my momma and tell my momma that I was ready to get out from over there. He didn't want me to use a phone an watched me on dat one. I was laughing and cryin' at the same time a lot so I just calmed down and put everything on the side and had to deal with my son, girl you know.

Den, he saw me walking he pick me up. He was nice like when I first met him. He must know I'm not in the state of mind that I was back in the day."

Talon allowed the pause, she could hear the memories reflecting throughout Jenni.

Jenni continued, "at anything he says I used to have to do now I would snap. It's different. It's not different for the best. But far from him putting his hands on me, him breaking me, and he say he won't, but I can't go back but goin' dis way it feels free but so much harder."

Talon thought and calculated. She softly inquired with sincere concern,

"Jenni, is your son, Zennu, his? Does your son Zennu go around him at all now?"

"Yeah, he stays with his son all the time, he would never do nuttin' to hurt any of his kids from all his fav's. He calls it trainnin' but he be getin' him stuff n' takin' him places, n' he wouldn't never hurt him". Talon knew that Jenni knew better. Jenni could be overwhelmed. This man ensured so much for himself when he impregnated them himself. Now, their trade for leaving the circumstances is a trade into tomorrow, the children. A worn through life for a life. How many will be in management and how many is he already siphoning off!

Jenni continued, "we gonna be, we gonna do a lot of things with the young kids at a stop the violence rally and I got a lot of people that is going to put in it. It's gonna be like a big thing, yep, so that's what I'm working on now." Talon interjected, "well, feel free to call anytime. You are not alone. But you can prove to yourself that you can as long as you try every day. Whatever you do not do is not failure. It is just another chance to succeed tomorrow." I'm so busy like forreal and when I be home girl I be so tired so basically like I try and do everything and try to promote, work on my website, like I need a manager. Aint nothin become nothin but like I aint bein beat for it neither. Right? Like, you see it right?"

Talon replied, "my approval is not what you need. As long as you have your own chance and do everything possible for your son then that is what matters. There is still much to consider and a lot of healing that needs to occur for you and your son. At least you have the second chance that you and your son needed. What you do with that is what you can decide each and every day. You decided not to do the family counseling, but you have stuck by your new job and kept your son in school. These are strong beginning steps. The modeling makes sense as he desired you to be physically appealing to everyone that came near but that no longer has to be the only meaningful measuring stick. You can begin to take GED classes and obtain a GED since he got you before you were even out of high school a long time ago. No matter what, at least your son can see a much happier and healthier person than the frail timid person I saw not long ago."

I could see you care and I aint gonna waste what you and my momma and everybody put into me.

I wanta ask you a question

okay

I got this guy that I started seeing, Inez,

umhumm

I found bite mark on his dick,

So, his phone went off when I usually sleep

it was someone who say they want to f his brains out, I say I was his woman and dey said so what, dey was married too. I say you must not love your husband cuz you all up on my man, dey said dey knew 'bout me but I was the woman and he was de man. He say no matter wat I thought Inez was full of a hunger that no one bitch could satisfy. He also said that Inez look down at me cuz he know that I was choked and other stuff before and say wat kinda woman would just take dat, and he see himself as so good because he temp timin' around my son so he see as a big deal instead of what it really say.

He aint say no sorry, I want to be honest, I will work through insecurity, flowers and butterflies. He say no female deserve a cheating partner but he feel I'm deaf to reality and easy and have a slow libido. He like the fake excitement of the first months of bein' wit a female. He say he don't mind still kickin' it but he wanna vet the next dude whenever dat hookup may come into play. What! So, he already sayin' that he wanna look the guy in the eyes that will fuck me with passion, see somethin' in me with dedication and respect that you know is more than you gave or will it be tragic that the truth is all I can see is unworthy through his eyes and will allow just the next person to come along that will check an empty box. Do you know anything that will increase my dopamine?

Giving Inez pleasure will not fix that he desires to use you until someone else rubbing his shoulders fits his next square. That warmth cannot get lit ever as long as the front door is always open. He will say that it is you because of who you were just recently stuck with and perhaps some of it is. Worse yet though, do you desire to remain with someone whose actions never match their words? They are telling you they do not desire to be trustworthy or provide a peace of mind foundation. There never is a guarantee no matter how short or how long you go. Elation comes either in brief conquering or long-term building. Treat yourself. And I realize that you will desire this treat to be something that he thought of but anyone who dares to desire to "vet" look a next person in the eye to say I had that first and only half ass cared, never cared about the absolute best of myself or Jenni, never desired to work through anything to reach the best level possible, I cannot find enough value in myself to value her or see a worthy validation in what we have shared, well, what twisted f'n shit is that! You may not be ready to own up to reality. But Inez is probably already intimately involved randomly with others, at least emotionally, so what room does that leave for you within his heart no matter how hard you try or that you are there? With that phone call, whatever you assume from it, do you wish to repeat where you have been or elevate to where you are going? How far are you willing to let him go or treat you if he does not hold enough value in himself to at minimum be respectful of what you have shared? Why do you want to see what is at the bottom of that rabbit hole if this is what is floating on the top? No matter how receptive or understanding that you are, he is looking forward to the day that he hands you off in an upstanding twisted was just passing the time of day with you until you moved on kind of way. What creates his enthusiasm beyond the limits he set forth will have little desire to be a shared emotion with you, even if you are present. Your strength of character will leave a desperate unhappiness that will persist until you face your decision of where you stand. Transgressions can be stepping stones and forgiven as life heals over. Perhaps leaving scars. Unless he changes his position, reaches for your hand in realignment and deciding that life is better approached with you than without you, stop predicting the unknown and judging your feelings upon fears or past that had nothing to do with you, grappling for an empty gesture instead the unlimited flood on-top of the mountaintop awaiting; you already know he is positioned not to be hurt, just you. You cannot invest into someone and not feel. Somehow though, many can put that into a box that they only bring out when they need it but not allow it to come from their core, without chance and without remorse. You may also desire to consider if your son should be intertwined with a person that is guaranteeing you they are going to toss you to the side when they are through, no matter how bright the future. Zennu has already gone through so much and has to decipher between what he has watched you go through to what his father is teaching him right now. I know you need love and support. Anyone that is this deliberate, and you called me, you definitely may desire to consider what occurs when you do not heed the true message and warning and he is tired of you, angry, or just owes a debt? For all that you are going through, consider counseling in order to be able to appreciate the strength of walking on your own two feet and lock up the love until someone will appreciate it sincerely. Most importantly, please, you still have time to be safe.

These are just my thoughts, no outrage or outpouring towards your budding relationship either way.

I desire the happiness of the person that was choked (you) as people sat around not caring. You deserve for someone to appreciate all of you for how and who you are. We all fail in some respect but "that person" should desire you to be their foundation as you are theirs. Tomorrow soars to levels on full display, on levels of joy and unforeseen dancing clouds that way instead of seething lingers and half interactions as you may choose to occasionally cross paths."

"He took my voice. He knows all my secrets."

"If you have to question it, even years later, then the honesty of it is that you do not have to question. You already know. Core can only connect to core. Either he decides that you're worth it to him even in his most unsettled waters and that he will very timidly reach and hold for wherever your water raft may float. Your tenacity probably was offered to his life because you can withstand whatever is to come, yet he may be still looking to build his own dam, trying to force waters to go in a direction that can never be forced no matter how bright that pond looks from all the way over here. You can shine and lovely, you do have a voice. You can find your voice through many other ways until you know you are letting go and walking through the door that he is leaving open with such a crass offering. You are stronger than you know. We often find out best selves when the person reflecting and interacting with us is positive and feeling uplifted. However, sometimes the match is not of their best self, true desires, nearly the same path, or perhaps yours. It is okay, although hurtful, to let go. One life Jenni, no do overs. Is he so valued that the time invested is worth it to you, to Inez, to Zennu? Just feel it through and whatever you decide, as long as everyone is safe and healthy then it is all good and you can always change it or challenge it down the road."

So, wat I say? I jus' thought someone like me and now I see I aint nothin noticeable.

Do not bomb out. There are physical responses to making these choices, but tomorrow is offered to all of us. You may be a flawless gem inside of a worn wrapper, but a gem nonetheless. Grant yourself no regrets, only stepping stones of experience and better expectations to the future.

Tell him,
Oh, my love, sweet love
It is now time to say goodbye
We've had our up's and down's
And a sweet rive of honey laid with white rose petals along the way
But somewhere between then and now
As we were playing hide n' go seek
Still and always finding out about each other
Playing these wonderful love games with each other
You can't find me, and I lost you
But somewhere between then and now
The river dried

You began to see a mirage
Relatin' to our relationship only just as a big tight pussy
Sayin'... just fuck it!

"Talon!" She belted out in a demanding laugh
"I be like, right!
I think that we at a check engine light, but Imma see if we can try some repairs. I know you say I need peace of mind and I won't forget dat you believe in me and I am always amazed dat y'all was able to get me like y'all did. Y'all got my back so
if dis car breaks down, I'll let ya know and I won't be stuck for Zennu's sake. You right, you right...."

"However, the truth lands, wherever your honestly lies, this line is open to you, and don't forget about all the other resources that goes beyond a shoulder that was offered to you as we got you."

"Yeah, I know. 'preciate it."

"Wobble it! With your head held high!"

"Hahaaaa, thanks! Bye."

"Remain well, Bye."

The absence of the synergy, the connective touch, the electricity that only flows through our currents, of course it would nice to be spiced a touch with a bit more elegance and atmosphere. Sometimes all he desires to do is to crash and readjust. It had been so long this time. What could feel like the attrap'reves hotel, transparent bubble pods in France and the Loisaba star beds, Kenya where nature surrounds them both in breathtaking moment freezing atmospheres. Since the planet ocean underwater hotel was only in a nearby state, and it is so differently exotic, it is extremely tempting also. To unify spirits, smiles, and to be one with nature and sunsets.

No barriers of the hustle and bustle or shyness although privacy ironically is on the extreme as the sunset kisses the forehead of the moment. These moments have caressed all over the region. Anywhere from Rhode Island, Savannah, Helen Keller, Disney, or Marriott Shoals 360 Grille, the elegant rotating restaurant that reminded me of Reunion Tower in Dallas, and so on and so forth. Only certain ones "freeze" as we found a new smile being out of our element and just breathing in the experiences.

Perhaps a true trip where we eat on the edge of the Cyclades, at the Narcissus, as the stunning sunset dances throughout the ocean scape view that is framed by the seductive romantic authentic restaurant's brick walls with open views. Perhaps from the longest detour that began with the Paracas Candelabra. A prehistoric geoglyph in Peru that mystically summons to its presence as if it were a fine wine. It is a cosmic energy world tree motif which is as breathtaking, connecting with nature, the underworld, the sky, the terrestrial realm, and unexplainable as the iconic symbolic Great Barrier Reef of Australia.

Even in this smile, the core erupts in craving to help those in need that may be present along the way.

But just as a father is supposed to bounce a child on her knees and not slam dunk them onto the couch, this will not be the wonderful exotic trip that De Jelle will return to.

Each moment has had its own flavor. Disney is different from the elegant fun 360 Grill that truly reminded of the original and irreplaceable Reunion Tower. The Ali center and museum day carried a different feel than Savannah. The bee keeper in the countryside with quaint towns was matched by Hellen Keller's hometown and all the integrity she exemplified. Nature, beaches, and cities, this lists only extends. So, what will be an appropriate momentarily welcoming location for this strong, confident, take charge, devastatingly debonair gentleman with expansive views yet a firm core.

Many women melt but not just at the sight of his looks, his wonderful teeth, the bulge in his pants but they also find themselves mesmerized with his magnetism, and mostly his intellectual caressment.

Although the cabins at Noccula Falls feel more appropriate, and the views are incredible, the

Seven Springs Lodge and Rattlesnake Saloon over twenty thousand acres feels plausible for this re-connective moment. Not exactly the most enjoyed Blue Lagoon in Iceland, but a desired connective location regardless. It is nestled at the cradled foothills of the Appalachian Mountains caressed by nature as if it were a suspended painting of times long ago. Although the idea of staying in a silo does not appeal since what has already been experienced throughout life would create a different impact just as having to consider animals in the road for many locations traveled would make it not the fascination nor connective touch.

Yet, as shoes are removed to feel the ground, or fingertips are run through the tips of the wheat, there is an inspiring humbled feeling when this site shares the Aboriginal Amerindian (Native Indian) shelters that also held the oldest Aboriginal remains found in Alabama to date. It was 8000 years old. There is a euphoria looking at someone with no makeup. There is a purity of happiness when time is only told by the light and warmth instead of any critical issues, loneliness, defeating all problems with a pure fresh moment only preserved and provided by nature suspended in time through the most simplest of caring. Since the location added the Rattlesnake saloon and it was named from a protective mother rattlesnake, that is relatedly appealing. Also, rattlesnakes can represent transformation, healing, dealing with unsettling difficult decisions. All conquering. The glove fitted location has been selected, and a few preparations were planned.

Truth be told, any location would be the spot of sweet molasses perfection. It does not matter where it really is. It matters only that everyone is safe and content. Everything else is a sun-kissed stream of beauty. It would be nice to repeat somewhere that offers decompression, changes and enhances he senses of the moment.

Everyone has that moment, that location. For Talon and De Jelle, it was Dogwood Manor.

The beauty that laid out before them, the Dogwood Manor, was a fantastic setting. It was one for clearing your head and breathing anew. The trees are grand. Old yet not too old, tall yet they don't reach for the sky. The swing in the trees is visible just as the bird baths are, simultaneous with as the leaves dance from the trees. The bed and breakfast air b and b sits in a way that yesterday was long ago and today is not just quite yet. Everything from its modest grandeur, the yellow walls, the angels representing a lost free spirit, to the painter's room that they stayed in all signified something with them, as if it were created for them or that their souls asked for it. Even if life encourages a park feel in one's daily life instead of a high-rise view, then this would still be a relaxing moment. The train depot of old across the street and the city just out of reach yet waiting for a delectable taste. This moment of connecting, this single night. The grounds, the air. And, In the magnolia room. It is another language not already written, now in great need to be spoken, the sparks of lightning shared but not spoken. The twinkles that sang songs of no words. The galaxies visited as they never left the room.

In the magnolia room. The broad sensually long petals are only a symbolism of what strong pulls, kind moments, bubbling overflowing illuminations, and energized explorations twisted from the time shared. The petals are at a peak and broaden to the pure middle that they protect the most and that appears to be the knotted spot of desire, viewed in the similarity of the sultry language and unforgettable enchanting moments that they shared. It was the synergy. For if it were not, the warm sparkling bathwater, with his special additives, in the claw foot tub would have only been a shared bath. The fruits shared were only for nourishment and not pleasure but each moment is engraved into happy enlightened memories. The power he held was not just his strong wrapped around Talon's back as he scooped her gently creating her hair to fall whimsically. The power was in his firm, secure, yet gentle confidence, his considerate nature, and viewing her laughter gleaming throughout his eyes.

He was majestic, powerful and kind. He watched her sleep. De Jelle gleamed, thinking, Talon was a bight interesting woman, someone he can relate rhythmically yet separately, someone he appreciates is there to share his time and enjoy him, also someone that can adore the outside as well as the events expressing etiquettes, someone who appreciates his judgments and thoughts as well as carrying her own. As she awoke De Jelle said to Talon "…. it's time to come up!" She heard his encompassing message of encouragement in De Jelle's very first statement of the day. "Gracias El gato, paco. chef intrépide, défenseur, (fearless leader, defender), messenger" Talon said in whimsical reply. It did not matter if the conversation of conjugation was of David Senna's firecracker artwork, Sheillah Charles whose art rivals professionals yet is only nine years old and whose heart and talent express determination and focus in an inspirational way, of the history of what they knew of the trees and the stories they may share as they glided throughout the grounds, leading to conversations of composting or recycling, and other wonderland random conversations. It created space for imaginations, it focused upon agreement or at least understanding view, and it focused themselves for every stroke of determination of stronger steps they were breathing deeper towards tomorrow as they had been re-energized and reminded together today.

He returned, the moment of reunification was of posters themselves. After a brief hello to the little excited toddler, they head to the chosen location. He will spend special time with the toddler soon and genuinely cannot wait.

Everything was set to perfect, even the slightest breezes and the brief mists of rain. It was warm, not stiff, just wonderfully warm.

When he reached out his hand, it sent out a sensuality of electricity. Walking into the saloon to eat, it wasn't the gentle breeze that was flowing tingling every nerve.

De Jelle wrapped his arms around Talon's tiny waist from behind her. DeJelle is big on no PDA so this was huge. He did not care who of the southern courteous strangers were looking. He gently moved Talon's hair to briefly expose the back of her neck. He bent down to kiss the back of her neck. The instant he did so Talon felt her leg shiver just a touch in her heels. DeJelle whispered, "I missed you". Talon thought, you are just horny, but smiled honestly within the melting Sprüngli or Ghirardelli moment. Walking to the table, Talon began to let the guard down that normally feels to be ready for danger at most moments. That sets the fine hairs on end and shortens endeavors because someone's quality time needs to be interrupted for their safety. De Jelle asked, "what do you think you would like to eat". Talon immediately lit up and slid right into it, "you". For a brief second De Jelle, the over talker, had no words; just a brief bright smile. "Are you very hungry" De Jelle asked as he knew her emotions were tied to her stomach. Talon removed her heel and rubbed her foot gently, for the man that was often uncomfortable with PDA, and she gently leaned in saying, "I'm just warning you dear, I am famished. Are you ready to feed me, all of me?" said with a smirkish grin. He said "Yeah! Let's go!" with a kiddish smile. Talon licked her lips, "I would love to slide underneath this table and overeat at the buffet that you have brought home." De Jelle responded with a raised eyebrow and an almost blush.

De Jelle looked at the menu and laughingly said "I am going to starve". "I know you eat for unification with your body and spirit, the owner is in agreement for a salad I brought, and look, they have french fries, fried mushrooms, we can do this, and if you feel like getting into a local mood and trying a desert we can try this deep fried cheesecake" Talon said half-jokingly and half attempting to keep the chosen atmosphere as a possibility. De Jelle responded, "I thought you were my desert" he said with a sheepish grin. "Mmm, and you are mine", she replied as his undertone indicated the differences from the eating preferences, and the very accurate engineered menu with no doubt to variety perfection towards the locale and the theme, would not impede the overall experiences.

Following the meal that contained lots of jovial moments, gentle hand touching, and no complexities of life outside of this moment. "Up for a walk?" Talon giddily asked. "I am up for a lot of explorations but sure, we can start with a walk" De Jelle responded smiling. The smile was that normally the walks were his idea. They talked about everything. It was so refreshing to just talk and touch at the same time as if the shared common space was the treat by its self. The way his eyes looked at her, the touches she shared with him. There is no recharging station that could ever compare to this moment. He sternly questioned her from his male dominating side of her faithfulness.

Talon retorted from her heart, that unity no much how much it modifies, is in accord as a whole. Not in fragmented parts. And that would not be fair to another as I have nothing to offer them as all of me already belongs to you.

DeJelle smirked in confidence yet he still cattle prodded the conversation just a little more although his soul knew that straying was not a part of her, yet he felt remiss not to inquire.

He repetitively inquired of a supplemental need that he witnesses time and time again where someone will just fill a certain part of a desire. Talon stood onto a rock and turned and faced him. She looked at him and said, "you always say how you admire my backbone, how you believe in me. I fight because of lost value of each individual, the responsibility that we as humans, as a one people, should have. It is a fight since the beginning of time. I only ask you to believe in us the way you believe in me or the amazing challenges that you achieve with unheard of fearless ambition. One's soul is a delicate and deliberate thing. I fight for that every day. With you, you do the tiniest gestures that harmonizes when you say you love me. To have several people to accommodate to one need, each one of those people connects to some space now not available and you really do not realize the magnitude to be broken into a puzzle. When we connect, we soar in an uplifting manner. I know you have fears, so do I. It's that effort despite your fears that makes me know that the time we share is valued by you, is needed by you, is desired beyond just some sexual connection, and the possibility of the future is as open as the future that we fight for every day individually. You vocally, myself quietly, yet the same fight. Tell me, what temporary person can fulfill any need that has already been painted in every corner?

There's no room remaining for them and whatever that they may have to offer we already are or can address to conquer. My artist, a person who knows how to caress one's heart, soul, body, future, and heal the past with only admiration and without questioning judgment, well those are unique qualities when combined. This soul is full, once you have had a meal of perfection, it remains with you, until offered again." De Jelle replied, "the space we create and enter is sacred, powerful, and even though there is no promise on tomorrow I only wish to see how bright this bloom will shine and how high we can soar together, I just wanted to know that I wasn't sharing with someone else. But if I am, I have watched you return to such a strong path in such a short time that I will only stand back and feel the heat of your rocket as you blaze off to new heights". They approached an area that should have been in a nature comedy movie. "My rocket prefers your fuel, nothing else will ever lift this rocket off the ground" she said with an exhaustive grin of where this was going.

"I heard of this group 'Sea to See'. They are visually impaired, but they bike incredible distances. They are athletes that see their impairments as a minor detail. They could have understood what limitations were expected with not being capable of having vision. Biking is a norm to know what is in your path and all the other barriers. They are not taking a test, they are recreating the exam. It would be nice if somehow, we can reach all of those that develop post trauma from the devastations that they were strong enough to survive but have been rewired. They have already used the strength to outweigh the probability of survival. The bikers without sight have more fierce vision to recreate the impossible. I would love to place those we help on top of the world like that within the power they already have despite that they think of themselves in a different light."

"To have blind ambition, you have to know your own inner light. When you go to do what you do, sometimes you must weave through many never seen, tornadoes of ghost winds to stop your helping those whose value is seen only as a purpose to someone else. That is from an inner light. If they are determined to not lose their flame, even if low, eventually when everyone pours their expertise offered into their direction perhaps they will cocoon and emerge stronger anew."

"When you keep talking, you get more handsome with every word." "You melt me with your vocalization of your mind."

But just as she said that, she must have been on the final stage of Total Knock Out, the television show. She was on a log and it began to rotate. She had to do a sloppy turn and jump that was not befitting of anyone that had a ring of flowers on her head from her love or that was combative at times during her day to day.

De Jelle jovially chuckled as he helped stabilize her. "I thought you were working out some as you were purifying your body from those opioids, so what were you really doing while I was gone". Talon threw a fake knife strike that he easily caught with his hand as she popped him in the knee gently as they both laughed. "I was doing research. The classics. Kama Sutra, want to test me?" she whispered into his ear as she trailed kisses from his cheek to his ear. "Only the deer and the horses to see us" she continued as she tried to sneak in a little more open connecting that was long overdue.

As they walked the property the moment just seemed to flush as a roller coaster going backwards. The sun was dancing upon the soft high grass that was politely hidden by the trees. They paused to admire the paintbrush of nature.

Right before them was a grotto, as if it was a nestled woman's pleasured spot waiting to be plunged into. Water is so connecting. De Jelle used this moment to re-connect spirits. It was not a carnal indulgence of momentary pleasure. They had already spoken and met with the minds often by phone and other means. This was the electricity from his words and touch to her soul and her responses to his heart and soul. They lied upon the wet mouth of this carved out hidden space. DeJelle laid the coat down that he had joked on Talon for even having said she always just had to have something to always bring with her, regardless of need. The coat that was conveniently handy would now need help, but it would be worth it.

Just as with fireworks, the smaller of the properties waterfall was just as mesmerizing. It fell from a shelf into a grotto overshadowing the mouth to a possible cave. The rocks can be seen throughout the water bed. It appeared too inviting. DeJelle stared into her eyes, she appreciated the moment. The foliage and trees danced through the surrounding cliffs and fertile grounds. The water was too thin and inviting. DeJelle said, "feel the breeze"

"Yes, but as much as I feel you"

He ran his finger as if he was mesmerizing her face all over again.

Talon laughed.

She jumped up and said, "I dare you!"

He rolled up his pants legs and followed her. As they waded in the water, they began flicking water at each other. It was a childhood highlight adult version. Talon sat in the cold water and leaned back. "I cannot believe you just did that!" DeJelle outburst laughingly letting her know that was a line he was not going to cross.

He saw her wet body through the clothes as she stood up. She was enjoying their interactions not to notice that he was still enjoying what was already his.

DeJelle took Talon out of the water leading her by the hand. They laid back in the soft grass, a little further back than before. He caressed her body while whispering to her. Even though it was DeJelle, she was not attacking him as she had mentally the entire time that he was gone. He kissed her attentively from neck to naval yet not as if it were a trail for traditional purposes. He saw her knee slightly bent and paused, kissing the bend of her knee. His hand was holding firmly upon the arch of her back. He took his time as if he were bringing a fine soup to a boil and his touches were as if they were lying on a bed of the petals of sweet roses. They both glanced around. No one was in sight. There are hundreds of acres and it has been a long time since the last touch. Her body tensed and shot a reminder of tingle as he scrolled his fingers across her stomach. She began to kiss him and run her hands every inch that she could reach. Talon took a sharp breath, a realization instinctively of how long it had been that her soul and body had connected with his. She felt DeJelle tense up, then slowly connect further into her arms, pressing his weight gently but deeper against her as his hardening cock rose pressing against her body. "Ohh mmmm" she said as he kissed along her neck glazing into her eyes. As he began to touch and trace her nipples, she could not help but grab his juicy firm ass. He circled all those nerves with his tongue and she felt all of her will power melt with each passionate moment. Any nearby sounds were inaudible. She ran her fingers across his hair as it draped over her. Yet most moments she felt out of control which was against every instinct of comforting nature for her. As he nestled his cock against her throbbing heating happy area awaiting to blanket him he leaned in and said, "I am the moon, you are the sun, I felt your vibrations even when I was away and could not wait for this magnetic moment with you once again, to just be in your arms once again", he took his finger and began to circle trace her throbbing happiness. "Ohh! She moaned, as she began to grind her hips in rhythm of his trace. As she kissed him and palmed his tight back of perfection, he pressed her hips gently as he removed her wet clothes down leaving nothing to the imagination. He placed their garments out onto a nearby rock, except for the coat that did not get soaking wet that they now laid upon. As he towered over her in all his glory, having laid the clothes nearby, Talon took advantage of the moment. She sat on her knees and ran her tongue around the head of his cock. She whispered to him, "feed me". It was a considerate symbiotic interactive dance. She had missed and craved this taste. The signature smell, touch, and taste that only belonged to him. She enjoyed the deliberate delicacy that was him. From each tender and sensationally fantastic location to clicking him with the back of her throat, she enjoyed each tender moment as much as he appeared to. They did not care the timing of it, nor any exotic bent across the wall moves that they have enjoyed. This was not about that. This was every note of music flocking throughout a silent moment. This was intertwining pure awe-inspiring synergy.

Talon gasps and moans inaudibly and DeJelle decides to guide her and re-take control of the situation. He said, "I was too close", she loves trying to make him cum that way but definitely also loves his lovemaking when he does not.

The reunification explorations continued, DeJelle kissed her down her leg, holding her firmly flat. Talon is a runner when it is something that she cannot control, and this is the ultimate connection with the ultimate force of letting go by someone else being in charge while touching every nerve in the body. DeJelle looks at Talon, as she relinquished any choice in the matter. DeJelle cupped her nipple into his hands overriding any instinct that Talon had. "Ohh!" she moaned. DeJelle slid his fingers actually touching the wet slit that was a fingerprint of familiarity for him. As Talon sharply took a breath he lowered his head licking and rolling in a rhythm that he knew would reach into her. Talon's body began to tense up as he slowly rubbed the folds, reached inside of her, rubbing in the same rhythm when he rotated between his sweet warm mouth and his rubbing. He knew he had begun to reach the climb that he was desiring when her breathing changed a little more erratic, and she said "wow, ohhh, wow, ohhhh... Uhhhhh" She moans. "Ohh! Yes, there pleeease, you psychic ..." As the pressure rose, so did she. She arched her back but then she began to push DeJelle away. She began to shake as the shattering feeling was overwhelming her. He used his Rhino stallion comforting control and continued on. She could only whimper "I'm about to...". He felt the tightness contracting onto his rhythmic fingers that he kept the same motions going. He ensured her that his head was out of the way by lying next to her gently, placing his rod right next to her, and kissing her, never slowing. She could not take the wonderful feeling of feeling him close at the base of her opening. Talon said, "no, no" as DeJelle just held her firmer. She exclaimed, "you are so deliciously hard!" and shuddered convulsing in deep breaths as her honey released involuntarily from her body leaving her in tremors.

After a few moments, as she felt him holding onto her tightly in his arms. She backs herself into him dripping but yearning for him, pressing her ass against his patient rock hard dick. She whispered, "you..." with a smile, turning her head to be mesmerized by his soul flooding through his eyes. She began to kiss him, as he kissed back with unspoken passionate words, she whispered to him, "I'd love to taste him again" he said, "now he tastes like us". She rubbed his glory against her slit once more before sliding down to visit, roll him throughout her mouth. She did wipe him a dab but fully enjoyed the harmony of her on him. She trailed her kisses back to him to whisper to him, "I am craving you", as she knew he instinctively had to feel the heat pulsing from her.

He grabbed her and flipped her like a feather to sit on top of him. As she slid him inside of her, he let out "Unnhhhh"! Talon then glanced to their surroundings for the first time since they began. Had it been an hour, three? Who knows. Time seemed to have slowed to an impossible passionate standing still while all of this began.

"Oh, crap!", she exclaimed, only not from the intimacy. Talon froze as a sudden ice sculpture clamping DeJelle with her legs. As she looked in the brush, she had a spread-eagle view of the most beautifully toned spread eagle legs balanced by a thick ass all attached to a moaning tall distracted woman. Her white dress was gathered around her waist as she was obviously propped for a personal view of the activities at hand. After the sudden shock of the momentary revelation was succumbed to, she realized how subdued and innocent the situation was. Although a person of fluid interest, Talon was not letting all of her guards down. The tall drink finally spoke as she realized that not only had she been discovered but the activities of re-connection had frozen, "I didn't mean to startle you, your interactive ballet of passion was just a turn on" she smiled. She continued in confidence, "would you like to touch me". Talon and DeJelle had already discussed where they stood on matters like this but to have it interject as intermission at this very moment was not just a discussion. DeJelle raised his eyebrow as if he were asking and obviously intrigued. But, the fascinating thing was, that is not what this particular moment was about. If she got off watching nature that is wonderful. And perhaps another time. But, the butterflies within this moment just did not include an unexpected gorgeous stranger. She began to moan and came with vibrant throws as she never moved her fingers from herself and her eyes from Talon and DeJelle. DeJelle enjoyed watching her thrust about and her hand move faster than any toy possibly could. Talon removed herself from DeJelle and began to recompose themselves. The three of them laid there looking at each other. Talon and DeJelle redressed as the stranger finally said, "Thank you for allowing me to intrude. I am Aaliyah-Natasha. I come here to escape. As many times as I have come here, I have never wandered onto such pleasure, this trip will be memorable thanks to you two." DeJelle laughed and began a brief light conversation of "what do you do, why do you need to escape". His eyes however were animated with repetitive replay of what was added to the evening that was not anticipated. DeJelle, Talon, and Aaliyah-Natasha walked back to the cabins and silos together.

Talon received a call.

"Yes?" Talon answered.

"Talon, if it is possible, we have a lady recovered who wants to return in because her child was in and not able to transition out and there is a location of high school age and college freshman age children that we would appreciate you to do the seminar with. Young adults understanding the value of their lives and holding ambition to not only utilize their lives but to protect themselves to the best of their abilities is incredibly important." The voice inquired and instructed from the other end of the call.

Talon respond. "What is the plan for the person with the mentality and focus to save her own but through such a drastic method of guaranteed sacrifice".

"Do what you do. Keep it unseen as usual."

DeJelle looked over and saw Talon's face. He said, not until tomorrow. She gave him the eyes. He knew she had to go. Tomorrow might be too late. Most of the time, it is very little that can have a full successful outcome despite the outpouring, the aggressive attempts, the full force and soaring foundation that Talon and others harmonize trying hard to overcome all obstacles one life at a time. Her expertise, her force, only to hope to succeed in a single life or few at a time for a second chance.

What the room looked like did not matter. The precious time shared was always held valued. When they departed from this location, renewed, De Jelle spent time valued as a family. The little tot leaped into his arms as if it had been every second of her tiny life. She rattled on about nothing that was everything. Every moment shared was delightfully deliberate and precious to them both. He looked into her eyes and wondered if he would ever be able to protect her enough and to teach her how to value herself the way that the future could receive her with everything positive that she would have to offer. They rode scooters, walked, gardened, talked, played, cooked, and just spent the time that was missed almost all in a moment or two. The point in time seemed to spin just as if it were a top on the floor, fast yet impossible. It was the best glimmer and sight to be seen.

Then, the tot, as she sat incredibly small in his wonderfully protective lap, asked him what he did as he painted the sky. He smiled at her and took a remix on stories of old. He told her that he rode in his chariot across the sky. Only, now, people plan to live in the sky. So, instead of cards into his chariot spokes, he decided to place paintbrushes. He had to be careful not to get any on the sun and the moon or definitely not the bright stars that she could point out and name. He dips the brushes in all different colors and then flies into the sky. These are the colors of the sunsets and sunrise. But just as the butterflies' dance with songs we cannot hear, he must paint day and night houses that we cannot see. There will be all sorts of buildings that will hold the educations of the future not even thought of so he thought he would bring visions of the Earth left behind, the fields that will still feed those long away, and the people that they will still love as we will love them, into images to flourish their imaginations and heart recollections. The tiny tot danced and imagined painting the sky into all sorts of colors along with places that cannot be seen. She grabbed the phone and pressed on the app that allows you to see the constellation that is near you. She said with all sincerity, "if we can see the map of where to go with our car, and this is the map of the stars so you don't hit any of them, then can you show me the map of the buildings that you paint so I can find all the best colors in the universe?" De Jelle laughed and smiled with the best hug for the tot. They danced around the room as she took out her markers and paint set and instead of painting another picture that she proudly brings home waiting for his return, she held up her paintbrushes towards the sky, where she now believed he rode his chariot to make the sky a better place.

De Jelle would soon have to return to yet another trip. Talon was the grounding for the group. She held the fort down between all his trips, kept life sensible for the tot and hopeful as she always remained connected to De Jelle as well. Talon enjoyed the tedious fundamentals so when DeJelle could decompress and dance upon the same star, even if momentarily, every moment is simply delectable for all. She now is not only working through the computer with very capable knowledge. She now has returned to her true calling, her Phoenix. She has conquered her own challenge which only made her ready to aggressively take on not only life as it approaches, but also take on the challenges of helping others retrieve their own lives back. To be able to make their own choices and to have the chances and opportunities that life presents to them. To make better, not just different of the same.

There is only one life given to each and every one of us and Talon feels that that is worth fighting for.

Would it not be wonderful if the tot grows to hold gifts from Talon and De Jelle into her own life that will reflect throughout whatever she decides to do and wherever life will carry her? Compassionate, foresight, helpful, defending, talented in her own right? Whatever message she may fight to send or stand for, it would be that she had the influence and the opportunity to fight. The beautification to remember and see what possibilities we all possess.

De Jelle viewed Talon as she returned. She had two bruises on her body and numerous marks that would be gone in a few days. It did not sit well. Yet, there was a smile as she could barely move. She whispered to him, "If I cannot take my pain meds, then what exactly do I take". All of this was said with the smile of success. Someone was able to have a little more help than they have ever had because of tonight. So, no matter what she was feeling like, and no matter what she had to face at home, this was worth it. He had found out that he had to go now for only another three months. He made a special tea, laid her down, and rubbed her in a special oil. Then, as he laid beside her he said, "I will not leave you, my body has to leave often, but I am here with you always." She smiled in comfort, knowing that in his heart, that is what he meant. It was consoling yet it was informative for Talon was aware that must mean that he knew he had to go. She ached throughout her muscles. She rolled over and touched his cheek. She kissed his neck, his cheek, and then him. She told him, "When you leave, you take a part of us with you. Please keep us safe, please make us whole again.". He inquired of her what happened to have her look like her body did. Talon laid there, and then she said, "I painted every blade of grass in the back yard a different color, did you see it last time", De Jelle smirked, gently touching her hair, and laid next to her. He said, "Oh yes, I saw that messed up job, we didn't know what had happened", they both laughed. He followed, "I know you just did that, so you could throw a party because I was gone". Talon followed, "No, the party was so that you would celebrate and be yourself while you were there, so you could hear the music. But, No one was dancing, we were just waiting for you to return." "Good one, good one, likely story" De Jelle let her off the hook. Smirking, Talon whispered a reminder to De Jelle. A true and vivid memory of a moment enjoyed. A moment they shared yet not the only moment and not nearly to be the last. She described how she will miss him, how she will reminisce when their bodies danced connectively, and her body shivered in rhythmic response with him while they both knew yet re-explored every inch of each other during every interaction of ecstasy.

They laughed and allowed their energies to sparkle as fireflies, playing without words. De Jelle wrapped Talon with an impenetrable defending and protective hug. He stared into her soul. "Do you feel me; do you really feel me". Her heart flooded open as her soul was already transparently braided with his "I do", Talon responded through a tender smile having felt all that his words did not have to say. They were connected. Not just for themselves but for those that they hoped to reach. In doing so, they hoped that their efforts would encourage others to do the same. They knew those that they worked with. They knew of others that were in the areas of expertise. It was for the next generations to be influenced and to not only take over but to overflow with empowerment beyond theirs. This was their shining light. This was the beginning foundation to Talon's Phoenix and De Jelle's continuous sharing of his exemplary shining light, internally overflowing.

The next morning, De Jelle was met with a wonderful sendoff of only hoping for his successes and quick safe return. As he was leaving, one of Phoenix's clients' ex-husbands with a position of authority, had sent out a statement to De Jelle and two other persons that were associated with members of the team that had assisted his ex-wife. He was furious and had only a dark agenda. As De Jelle had often seen the incredible bond and relationship with Talon and tiny tot as a wonderful investment, a sun and moon meeting that connects and creates its own unique energized force. This man had only viewed his wife as a trophy, an asset of sorts. He kept her locked most days in a basement wing of the house. It was more than adequate. His expectations of her removed all choice. The statement from him to De Jelle was borderline on all that it said but it definitely had the undertone of "return my 'property' or else I will result in removing yours". De Jelle was rattled. He was leaving, and the message was already received as the communication was shared with the targets; not the persons who helped. It was also realized what this meant for the tiny tot, or anyone else that may share their path. With his resources, it was no wonder how he retrieved the information that is normally not as easily found. For him to rattle the whole team was an interesting tactic. Yet, why did he not feel there were other resources? and if the point was to remove someone that helped his 'property' who in turn was locked in a basement, an entire wing or not, his actions were aggressively abusive and did not help his goal.

Talon reassured De Jelle that nothing would come of it and that they had this under control. They reviewed the precautions that would be taken and ensured him that she was on it. Once again, the fight was no longer for just others, now it was for her team and those that she cared for all in one blow. The talons were coming out and the person who signed that letter had no idea what he was in for. Yes, he may be upset, but he took very serious steps already to prove that protection was necessary. Talon was strategic, and not worried in the least. This was not a sneak attack. She tucked away the tiny tot to the safest level possible. She reassured De Jelle, and then she met the members of the team that knew this had to be handled. Not just for them but also for the replacement that this sort of person would repeat his habits with. They went to do just that. The Phoenix was on fire.

*… waiting for De Jelle to return…*

*Shhh…CONFESSIONS…The Best LOVE Story, From The Inside Out*

Printed in the United States
By Bookmasters